Sabrina looked beseechingly
at her campers.

"I want to see if we can get through one meal without something terrible happening. Okay?"

The girls were already ignoring her, as usual. As they chattered and argued, they weren't exactly quiet, but they weren't behaving any worse than the campers at the other tables. Sabrina scooped up a spoonful of baked beans and gulped it down.

Suddenly the girls at her table became deathly quiet. They were all staring at her. Sabrina didn't know what was wrong until an entire bowl of Jell-O landed on top of her head. As the lime green gelatin oozed down her neck and under her shirt, she looked up to see Jill's angry, tearful face.

Everyone in the huge hall was quiet, and they were all staring at Sabrina, wondering what she would do.

The deathly silence was interrupted by a loud cry.

"Food fight!" screamed Patty.

Sabrina, the Teenage Witch™ books

Available from ARCHWAY Paperbacks

Sabrina The Teenage Witch™

Prisoner of Cabin 13

John Vornholt

AN ARCHWAY PAPERBACK
Published by POCKET BOOKS
New York   London   Toronto   Sydney   Tokyo   Singapore

AN ARCHWAY PAPERBACK *Original*

An Archway Paperback published by
POCKET BOOKS, a division of Simon & Schuster Inc.
1230 Avenue of the Americas, New York, NY 10020

ISBN: 0-671-02115-X

First Archway Paperback printing June 1998

10 9 8 7 6 5 4 3 2 1

AN ARCHWAY PAPERBACK and colophon are
registered trademarks of Simon & Schuster Inc.

Printed in the U.S.A.

IL: 5+

To Jean Reich

Prisoner of Cabin 13

Chapter 1

☆

☆

From the shadows stepped a handsome young man wearing a black leather jacket. He had smoldering eyes, and he needed a shave. The beautiful blond woman gasped and tried to escape from him, but there was nowhere to run on the balcony of her penthouse. He grabbed the train of her elegant evening gown and roughly pulled her toward him.

As the woman struggled in his arms, Treg growled, "It's no use, Marlene! We were meant to be together—"

"Wrong," muttered Sabrina, who was still in her pajamas, lying in bed and watching TV. "Marlene doesn't need a loser like you. What about Roger?"

She pointed her finger at the TV, and musical notes tinkled in the air. At once Marlene was in the arms of the dashing Roger, not the grungy Treg. She

1

didn't look any happier, however—she just looked surprised and confused.

"Roger, what are you doing here?" asked Marlene, pushing the rich industrialist away. Looking embarrassed, she fluffed her hair.

Roger, being a gentleman, let her slide out of his grasp. He pleaded, "I've always loved you, Marlene. Let me prove it to you!"

"But you're married to my *sister!*" shrieked the blond woman, aghast.

Sabrina frowned. "Ooh, I forgot about that." With another point of her finger, Marlene found herself in the arms of Mark, her decent and loyal ex-husband.

"Mark!" she shouted in amazement and relief. "What are *you* doing here?"

He looked confused, too. "I don't know. I thought I disappeared in a boating accident on the Amazon."

"Bummer," muttered Sabrina.

A knock sounded on her bedroom door. "Sabrina!" called Aunt Hilda's voice. "May I come in?"

"Sure!"

Hilda strode into the room, dressed in bright pink shorts and a fluffy summer top. "Are you doing something to the television?"

"Just fixing this silly soap opera," explained Sabrina with a shrug.

"Well, I happen to *like* that silly soap opera," groused Hilda. "And I like Treg better than those other guys."

2

She pointed at the TV. In a flash Marlene was back with Treg, who wore a leather jacket and always needed a shave.

"Marlene!" he cried gratefully as if he had been locked in a dark closet for several hours. He hugged her desperately, and she tried to keep him from mussing her hair and gown.

"That's better," said Hilda, nodding with satisfaction. "He'll do until her true boyfriend, Cliff, gets back from the war. You know, Sabrina, you really shouldn't try to change soap operas—they're already too confusing."

"I know," said Sabrina. "But now that it's summer and school's out, I'll have time to catch up on all of them!"

Her fun-loving aunt frowned and sat on the edge of her bed. "Is that how you're planning to spend the whole summer? Watching soap operas?"

"No," said Sabrina defensively. "Maybe I'll watch a few game shows, some rock videos."

"No, that's not what I meant. Are you going to *lie* around all summer?"

"I suppose I could *fly* around," answered Sabrina with a grin. She wiggled her finger and levitated a foot off the bed. "Now where did I leave my vacuum?"

"It's in the linen closet," said Hilda. "But you know what I mean. You can't just veg out all summer long. You're a teenager—you need to be *active.*"

Sabrina frowned and dropped back onto her bed.

"I'm sorry, Aunt Hilda, but there's nowhere to go. All my friends are away on vacation or have summer jobs. Look at Harvey—he's in Europe with his parents, meeting a bunch of French and Swedish girls—" The teenage witch snapped her fingers. "Hey, that's it! I can go there and ruin his vacation!"

"No, no," said Hilda, shaking her head. "That might be fun for a while, but it's not fair for him and his parents. They've really been looking forward to that vacation. Besides, Harvey is not the problem. You're the problem. Even if your friends are busy, you can't just mope around the house all summer. You said that some of your friends have jobs—*you* could get a job."

Sabrina rolled over and sighed. "A job? You mean like serving fast food? Minimum wage? Gimme a break!"

"Money isn't the only reason to get a job," answered Hilda. "You could get a job to contribute something to society, to help people. Your aunt Zelda has a very important role in the science community, and I have my art and my music. Working hard at something makes you feel good about yourself."

"I'll think about it," promised Sabrina, turning her attention back to the TV. "Look! Treg just threw Marlene off the balcony!"

"What?" Hilda whirled around to see for herself, and Sabrina burst out laughing.

"Just kidding."

"Very funny," muttered Hilda. "Why don't you get out of your pajamas and *do* something? You could clean Salem's litter box."

"Whatever," said Sabrina, barely listening to her. "I'll stop being a slug just as soon as this program is over."

Aunt Hilda sighed and walked out of the room.

That night Hilda was trying to cook dinner, using real cooking, but her mind kept drifting back to Sabrina. Her sister, Zelda, sat at the kitchen table, reading a book.

Salem, a handsome black cat, sat on the counter, his tail swishing back and forth. Nothing made the familiar as happy as watching food being prepared. The cat even hummed contentedly to himself— some forgotten opera.

Hilda looked at the cream sauce bubbling in a pot on the stove. Even though she had a magical cookbook to help her, she kept making mistakes in the recipe. She picked up an egg and started to crack it into the bubbling mixture.

"No, no!" complained the cookbook. Actually it was a picture of a chef on page 168 who berated her. "You *fold* two eggs into the sauce. Don't you know how to fold eggs?"

"Sure, I can fold eggs," snapped Hilda angrily. "Watch this!"

She wiggled her finger, and two eggs hovered over the cookbook, cracked open, and dropped their yucky contents onto the pages. The sputtering chef was drowned in gooey whites and yolks. With a loud whooshing noise, the book snapped shut.

Aunt Zelda shook her head and remarked, *"You are going to have to take that book back to Drell's library."*

Hilda sighed. "I know I'm grumpy, but I'm worried about Sabrina. Since school let out for the summer, she just lies around and sleeps. It's not healthy. I think she's depressed."

Salem snorted derisively. "Then all cats must be depressed. Lying around and sleeping—sounds perfectly normal to me."

"It's not normal for Sabrina," hissed Hilda. "All of her friends are away on vacation or working—she's bored. She needs something to occupy her, like a summer job."

Zelda adjusted her reading glasses. "Then let's see what's in the newspaper." She held out her hand, and the want ads of the local newspaper popped into her manicured fingers.

After reading a few seconds, Zelda frowned. "Burger flipping might be okay for some people, but Sabrina needs a job that will challenge her."

"Pick something *fun*," said Hilda enthusiastically. "We still want her summer to be enjoyable."

"Of course." Zelda read some more, then the elegant witch smiled with satisfaction. "Here's just the thing! Didn't her mother always tell us how Sabrina loved to go to summer camp when she was a child?"

"Yes!" said Hilda excitedly.

"Well, here's an ad for a local summer camp, and they need camp counselors! Lots of fresh air, exercise, and adorable children. What could be better for Sabrina than that?"

"Oh, that does sound perfect!" agreed Hilda.

Salem grumbled, "Camp? As in sleeping *outdoors* in the leaves and dirt. Yuck! Give me room service."

"Well, I'm sure they don't sleep outdoors," answered Zelda, "at least not every night. There's an address where she's supposed to send a résumé with her work experience."

"But Sabrina doesn't have any experience as a camp counselor," said Hilda worriedly. Then she grinned. "But we can fix that."

Hilda pointed to the table, and a perfectly typed résumé appeared in a flash. Both women leaned over the sheet of paper and studied it.

"Two years of experience?" asked Zelda doubtfully.

"Right," said Hilda with a frown. "Why not make it *three?*" The exuberant witch zapped the sheet of paper, making numbers and words jump around the page like fleas. "And I'll make the camps where she worked real fancy. Only the *best* camps."

Salem yawned. "Oh, why don't you just put her in *charge* of the camp?"

Hilda looked at the cat for a moment, unsure whether he was kidding or not. "No, that might be too many headaches. This is good enough."

7

"Lying on a résumé is against my better judgment," warned Zelda.

"Thank goodness we have *my* judgment," replied Hilda. "Now to put Sabrina's résumé on the top of the pile." The witch wiggled her finger, and the sheet of paper lifted off the table, shot across the room, and disappeared up the vent over the stove.

"Well, that takes care of that," announced Zelda. "If she doesn't get a job with *that* résumé, there's no justice in the world."

"I feel better already," said Hilda with a grin. She looked at the cream sauce curdling in the pot on the stove. "Anybody want to send out for pizza?"

Glumly Sabrina tightened the belt on her jeans and buttoned her shirt. It was time that she got dressed and went down to see if she could help with dinner. But how could you help a witch make dinner, except to stay out of the way? Oh, well, she should at least go downstairs and visit with her aunts and her cat.

I really am being a slug, she thought. All winter long, she looked forward to the summer, and now it was here. How did she react? By becoming a hermit and staying cooped up in her room. There were a thousand magical realms she could visit—plus the mall—but it all seemed so pointless without her friends.

Oh, she could create new friends with Man-Doh or some other magic, but they weren't the same as *real* friends. Sabrina wished she could see Harvey's sweet smile or hear Valerie's goofy laugh. But Harvey was away and Valerie was working. She wondered how much TV she could watch, and how many books she could read before she went crazy.

The telephone rang, and Sabrina let somebody else answer it. Normally, she would have rushed to pick it up, but she knew it wasn't for her. She listened, but nobody called her name—it wasn't for her. Sabrina sighed, slouched out of her room, and headed down the stairs.

When she reached the kitchen, she saw Aunt Hilda on the phone, nodding and smiling. "Yes, tomorrow will be fine," said Hilda. There was only one thing odd about this—she was using Sabrina's voice.

"Good-bye," said Hilda. She hung up the phone and grinned at the teenager.

"If you made a date for me," Sabrina warned, "he'd better be cute."

"Oh, that wasn't a new boyfriend," replied Hilda. "That was your new *boss.*"

"I don't remember getting a job, so how could I have a new boss?" Sabrina cringed, fearing that her aunts had done something crazy, as usual. "I'm going to go upstairs to my room, then come back down, and we'll pretend this conversation never happened. Okay?"

"But, Sabrina, you'll like this job," Aunt Zelda assured her. "We picked it out especially for you."

Sabrina sank down into the chair beside Zelda.

"I appreciate it, but I don't think we have the same taste in jobs."

"We know what you like," said Zelda with a laugh. "How does this sound: 'Sabrina Spellman, camp counselor'?"

Sabrina blinked at her aunts, then a smile crept across her face. "Camp counselor? That's sounds all right. I always liked summer camp. I'm really good at sewing moccasins."

"Yes, we know," said Hilda excitedly, "and Camp Bearclaw is only two hours away. They want you to start tomorrow. Another counselor named Jill is picking you up in the morning and will drive you there."

"I should be mad at you," said Sabrina, "but maybe this will be fun. How exactly did I get this job?"

"You sent them a really great résumé," answered Zelda. "Hilda exaggerated your experience a little bit. Don't worry about anything—they love you already."

"I don't know," said Sabrina doubtfully. "What if I don't like it?"

"It's a coed camp," added Hilda. "There will be boys and boy counselors."

Sabrina jumped to her feet. "I've got to start packing! I'll need clothes, a bathing suit, a flashlight, blankets, and some bug spray. Do you know what I'm going to be doing there?"

"You'll be watching a cabin full of ten- and

eleven-year-old girls," answered Hilda. "How hard can it be?"

"Yeah." Sabrina grinned. "I used to be eleven. How hard can it be?"

"That's the spirit," said Zelda. "You go up to your room and pack, and we'll call you when dinner's ready."

"Thanks! I love you guys." Sabrina gave each of her aunts a big hug, then charged out of the room. Salem padded after her.

Salem watched Sabrina's frantic packing thoughtfully. The witch's familiar couldn't figure out why Sabrina was so excited.

"You need all that junk to sleep outside?" asked the cat suspiciously.

"I'm not sleeping outside," said Sabrina with a laugh. "A sleep-away camp is not the same as camping in the woods. Most of the time we'll sleep in a cabin."

"Will the cabin have heat and air-conditioning?"

"I doubt it."

"Will you have bathrooms?"

"No, we'll probably have outhouses."

The cat shivered. "It sounds like the Middle Ages to me."

"Oh, you'd like it," said Sabrina. "You get to have fun all day, make arts and crafts, and take nature hikes. You could probably catch all kinds of field mice."

"Have you ever *eaten* a field mouse?" asked
Salem.

"Um, no, can't say that I have."

"Me neither, and I intend to keep it that way."

"Cats aren't invited, anyway," declared Sabrina.
She stuck an extra sweater into the duffel bag and
nodded with satisfaction. "There's room left, but I
think that's all I need. I'm going down to see what's
for dinner."

Whistling cheerfully, Sabrina strode out of the
room, leaving Salem all alone.

"Cats aren't invited," he sniffed. "Who wants to
go to her crummy old summer camp, anyway?
Field mice and outhouses, indeed!" He eyed her
open bag. "Indeed . . ."

☆

Chapter 2

☆

Sabrina! Your ride is here!" shouted Aunt Zelda, peering out the window. Morning sunlight streamed through the blinds into the living room, which looked like a room in a normal house, even though this wasn't a normal house.

Sabrina came running down the stairs, her bag slung over her shoulder. She was dressed in T-shirt, shorts, and her sturdiest tennis shoes. Both Hilda and Zelda were waiting by the door, ready to see her off. She hugged them excitedly.

"I can't believe I'm really going!" exclaimed the teenager. "Whoo-hoo! This is *so* cool. Thanks."

"Our baby is leaving home." Hilda sniffled, dabbing at her eye with a handkerchief.

"It's only for a couple of weeks," said Sabrina, "and I'll only be two hours away. Faster by vacuum."

"Have a good time," said Zelda, "and send us thought-grams every day. Do you have everything?"

"I think so." Sabrina looked around, puzzled. "Where's Salem? I want to say good-bye to him."

Hilda sniffed. "He's probably too upset to see you leave."

"I doubt that," said Sabrina. A horn sounded, and she started out the door. "Tell him I said good-bye."

"Have fun!" called Zelda.

Sabrina walked down the drive toward a station wagon that had a claw logo on the side and the words "Camp Bearclaw." Behind the wheel sat a very pretty dark-haired girl who looked to be a couple of years older than Sabrina.

"Hi!" she said, climbing in. "I'm Sabrina Spellman."

"Yes, I know," replied the dark-haired girl. "Super Counselor."

Sabrina gulped. "Super Counselor?"

"Well, we don't receive many résumés like *yours,*" replied the girl.

"I can imagine that," said Sabrina half-joking. *Yikes! What did my meddling aunts write about me?*

"I'm Jill," said the driver. "Even though you've worked in all those fancy camps on Long Island, you're still a first-year counselor at Bearclaw."

"I understand that," answered Sabrina, thinking

fast. "In fact, I'm willing to act like this is my *first* job at a summer camp."

"Good, then we won't have any problems." Jill put the car in reverse and backed out of the driveway.

As they drove through the quiet, tree-lined streets on a beautiful Saturday morning, Sabrina tried to ease some of the tension.

"Can you tell me anything about Camp Bear-claw?" she asked.

"Well, it's not as big or as fancy as the places you worked before," said Jill, "but it's a nice little camp. Arthur is very well organized."

"Arthur?"

"Arthur Rimbard, the camp director. You sent him your résumé."

Sabrina laughed nervously. "Oh, of course. *That* Arthur."

"For example," said Jill, "we keep records on all the campers. We know which ones were well-behaved and which ones were a problem last year. To make it easy on everyone, we put all the problem campers in the same cabin."

"Oh, that makes sense," replied Sabrina, thinking it really didn't.

"We also have lots of activities and competitions. Arthur is a big believer in keeping the campers busy."

"What about having fun?" asked Sabrina.

Jill gave her a fishy look. "Who said camp was fun? It's hard work."

"Of course," said Sabrina, nodding seriously. "Hard work."

"It was perfect timing that we got your résumé," added Jill. "We really needed another experienced counselor right away. The campers will arrive by bus later this afternoon, and there won't be much time to get settled in. We'll have a meeting with Arthur, then get to work."

"Right," said Sabrina, sounding more confident than she felt. "Get to work."

Her gloomy mood lifted as they left the city behind them and drove along a winding country road. Purple and green mountains loomed ahead of them, and the air smelled fresh, like blossoms and evergreen trees. Soon the car was climbing steadily into the mountains, and Sabrina had a feeling that everything was going to be all right. At least Camp Bearclaw was in a beautiful setting.

Sabrina looked at the girl sitting beside her. Jill was all-business, but she had the right attitude. For the counselors, this was a job, not fun and games. Sabrina hoped that they wouldn't find out that she was a fraud and had never worked as a counselor before. Of course, she could use a spell if she needed to, but she hoped she wouldn't need to.

There was still one topic she wanted to discuss. "What are the guys like? I mean, the counselors."

For the first time, Jill smiled. "They're not bad, if you like handsome, muscular guys who are all tan from working in the sun."

"Nah," scoffed Sabrina, "I like wimpy guys who are all pale and pasty."

Jill's smile faded, and her dark eyes narrowed. "You won't have much time for romance, but if you do, there's one guy who is off-limits."

"Uh, who's that?"

"His name is Mitch. Stay away from him."

Sabrina frowned. "Why, is there something wrong with him?"

"No, he's *perfect.*" Jill's stern expression made it clear why Sabrina should stay away from him.

"So . . . he's taken?"

"He doesn't know it yet, but he is."

Sabrina just nodded and looked out the window. She couldn't believe it. This was her first summer without any parents or aunts hanging around. There was nobody from home to check up on her—she was all by herself. *This is what summer camp is all about, being independent.* Sabrina smiled and watched the beautiful scenery roll past her.

It's going to be a great *summer!*

Jill steered the car down a dirt road, and Sabrina sat up and looked around. She felt as she had when she went away to camp for the first time—excited and a little scared. They passed a cute log cabin on the left and a baseball diamond on the right.

"That's Arthur's cabin," said Jill. "He's the only one who gets a private cabin." She pointed out three larger buildings, all painted red, like barns.

"That's the Recreation Center, the Lodge, and the Dining Hall. The Nature Exhibit is in the Rec Center, and the Nurse's Office, Staff Room, Camp Store, and Director's Office are in the Lodge."

"Where are the cabins?"

"Back in the woods. You have to take the trails to get to them."

"Cool!" exclaimed Sabrina.

Jill shrugged. "It's not so cool when your flashlight runs out of batteries in the middle of the night. On your left are some more places you'll be spending your time."

Sabrina looked out the window as they drove past a swimming pool and a basketball court. Then Jill pulled into a parking lot that was hidden behind some shrubbery. There were only a few cars parked there, and most of the spaces seemed to be for buses. Sabrina jumped out of the car and grabbed her bag even before Jill had turned off the engine.

Sabrina filled her lungs with delicious pine-scented air as she gazed around at the towering evergreens and the bright blue sky. Through the trees she caught sight of a streak of dark blue, and she heard a gurgling sound. "Is there a river here?" she asked.

"A small one," answered Jill, grabbing her own bag. "We have to have a place to hold canoe races. I bet those fancy camps where you worked before had both rivers *and* lakes."

"Some of them had oceans," claimed Sabrina.

She was getting a little tired of Jill, and she was looking forward to meeting some other counselors.

Near the swimming pool was a squat red building. "What's that?" asked Sabrina.

"Oh, that's the locker room—where there are showers and rest rooms."

Sabrina smiled. "Salem would be glad to hear that."

"Who?"

"Just a friend of mine. He was worried that we would only have outhouses."

"We have those, too," said Jill. "Up by the cabins. Just let your nose lead the way."

Sabrina's duffel bag suddenly shifted and started to slide off her shoulder. She hoisted it higher onto her back and looked around, taking in the idyllic setting. Camp Bearclaw was a little rustic, but it still felt great to be out in the woods and the fresh air.

"It's so peaceful—"

A whistle shrieked, making her jump. Sabrina whirled around to see a gangly man dressed in sparkling white shorts and T-shirt striding toward them. He was wearing glasses and looked more like an English teacher than a camp counselor.

"That's Arthur," whispered Jill.

He blew his whistle again and motioned toward two young men on the basketball court. "You counselors! We have a meeting in five minutes!"

"Yes, sir!" they shouted back. Quickly they hustled off the court and ran toward the Lodge.

Without pausing for a moment in his frenetic pace, Arthur Rimbard rushed toward Sabrina and Jill. He was like a bundle of energy as he kept tugging at the whistle around his neck.

"Jill!" he said with a grin. "Is this our Super Counselor?"

"This is Sabrina Spellman," answered the dark-haired girl. "Whether or not she's a Super Counselor, we'll find out."

Arthur looked Sabrina up and down, as if she were a piece of furniture. "I was expecting someone older, bigger."

"I have hidden talents," said Sabrina, thinking of a few magical ways she could shut Jill up. She held out her hand. "I'm pleased to meet you, Mr. Rimbard."

He gripped her hand and pumped it. "Call me Arthur. I'm certainly glad you're here, Sabrina. We really need someone with your experience. I don't think Camp Bearclaw will be as exciting as some of the places you've worked, but we try to run a tight ship."

"Just think of me as a first-year Bearclaw counselor," said Sabrina with a nervous smile.

Arthur frowned. "I've got lots of those already. I need a pro like you." Something in the woods caught his eye, and he blew his whistle before Sabrina could cover her ears.

"William!" he shouted. "Have you painted those lines on the volleyball court?"

An older man was shuffling through the woods. "I'm on my way!"

Arthur shook his head. "William is a good handyman, but he's a little slow. Come on, let's go to the Lodge for our meeting."

As they walked briskly up the road toward the large red buildings, Arthur remarked, "I'm sure I don't need to lecture an experienced counselor like you on the rules."

Sabrina gulped. "Well, I am new at *this* camp."

"Spoken like a true professional," said Arthur. "The main rules are: no food in the cabins. Food invites animals, and we don't want *any* animals in the cabins. No writing or carving on the walls. No boys in the girls' cabins, and no girls in the boys' cabins."

"Uh, that makes sense," said Sabrina.

"All the rules and regulations are in the handbook," added Arthur. "I'll give you a copy, and you can memorize them by tomorrow."

Not another handbook, thought Sabrina. She'd had enough problems with the Witch's Handbook and the Quizmaster. Studying to get her witch's license should make studying a camp handbook a snap.

Suddenly Jill stopped, and her eyes went all glassy as she stared into the distance. "Mitch."

Sabrina followed her gaze and saw a tall young man with dark brown hair striding toward them. He carried paint buckets in both hands, causing the muscles in his arms to ripple as he walked. Sabrina thought about the actors in that soap opera she had been watching, and Mitch was more handsome than any of them. She could see why Jill was drooling.

But Arthur looked angry. "And where are you going?"

Mitch glanced shyly at Sabrina. "I was going to give William a hand with the painting."

"That's *his* job," insisted Arthur. "Don't you have enough to do without trying to do everyone else's job?"

"But he's an old guy," said Mitch apologetically. "I thought I could give him a little help."

He's gorgeous and a sweetheart, too, thought Sabrina. *No wonder Jill is crazy about him.* His blue eyes met hers, and she couldn't do anything but smile sheepishly.

"This is Sabrina, our new counselor," said Arthur. "Even though she's young, she's had lots of experience."

"Great!" exclaimed Mitch. "Welcome to Camp Bearclaw, Sabrina."

"Thanks. I'm glad to be here."

"Mitch," said Arthur, "after the meeting, you can show Sabrina around the camp."

"I'd be glad to," he answered, his blue eyes sparkling.

Jill cleared her throat. "But *I* can show Sabrina around. Or we both can."

"Jill, I need you with me to meet the campers,"

22

said Arthur. "Mitch can do it—he's doing everything else. Take that paint to William and hurry back to the meeting."

"Yes, sir. See you later, Sabrina, Jill." With a cheerful smile, the young man hefted his paint buckets and hurried off. Sabrina and Jill both turned to watch him go.

Yes, thought Sabrina, *it's going to be a good summer.*

Chapter 3

Sabrina followed Arthur and Jill into the Lodge and came face-to-face with a huge bear, rearing up in front of her! She shrieked and jumped back.

Jill laughed at her reaction. "That's Henry, our mascot," she explained. "He's stuffed, not alive."

"He's dirty and moth-eaten, too," said Arthur with disgust. "I'd like to get rid of the bear, but the campers love him."

Sabrina studied the stuffed bear and realized that he was pretty old. He must have guarded the Lodge since the day the camp first opened. "Is that how Camp Bearclaw got its name?" she asked.

"No, the camp gets its name from Bearclaw Rock," said Arthur. "That's where we have our fire circle—where we do sing-alongs and have our closing ceremonies. You can leave your luggage here in the lobby." The camp director spotted some other counselors and hurried off to greet them.

Jill lowered her voice to say, "Bearclaw Rock is also a good place to go when you want to be alone. It's at the end of a long hiking trail."

"I'll have to see it sometime," said Sabrina.

"Oh, you will," added Jill.

Sabrina dropped her duffel bag in front of the bear and followed the others into the staff room. There must have been twenty-five counselors, and there weren't enough chairs for everyone to sit. A few of the counselors were older adults, but most of them were in their late teens or early twenties.

Arthur strode to the front of the room, and Sabrina worried that he would blow his shrill whistle. Instead he held out his hands and grinned. "Counselors and staff, welcome to Camp Bearclaw!

"I see a lot of familiar faces here, and also some new faces. As you know, the campers will start arriving in less than an hour, so we don't have any time to waste. If you want to get to know each other, do it on your own time."

He picked up a clipboard and studied it. "Our first session is a week long, and it's all ten- and eleven-year-olds. We've filled almost every bunk, so we're going to have to be efficient. *Very* efficient. Your cabin is your primary responsibility, and you will also be scheduled as craft teachers, coaches, nature guides, and table counselors."

Sabrina turned to Jill to ask what a "table counselor" was, then she remembered that she should already know that. After all, she was Super Counselor. *Oh well, I'll find out soon enough.* Her eyes scanned the gathering until she found Mitch, who was listening intently to the director. He was easy on the eyes.

Arthur went on with his pep talk for a few more minutes. He told them that they had to set a good example for the campers, and that counselors could get fired for breaking the rules. *What about sending in magical résumés?*

Finally the director picked up a box full of manila envelopes. "Here are your cabin and work assignments, plus a list of your campers. When I call your name, please come and get your envelope. I also have a stack of handbooks, if you need one."

Sabrina hoped she would be a crafts teacher, because that was really the only thing she remembered from going to camp as a kid. She watched nervously as the other counselors received their assignments, until finally her name was called.

When Arthur gave Sabrina her envelope, he also gave her a handbook. It was about two inches thick. "You have to memorize that by tomorrow," he reminded her.

"Yes, sir," answered Sabrina with a brave smile.

There was a lot of chatter as the counselors discussed their assignments.

"Cabin seven!" said one happy counselor. "All right!"

"Cabin nineteen," muttered Jill. "That's one of the farthest ones. What did you get, Sabrina?"

"I'll look." She opened her envelope, removed a stack of papers, and glanced at the first sheet. "Cabin thirteen."

There was silence all around her, and Jill smiled.

"Let me see," said Mitch, looking over her shoulder. "Yeah, it says thirteen."

"What's the matter with thirteen?" asked Sabrina. "Is the cabin haunted?"

"Not at all," said Mitch with forced good cheer. "It's one of the newer cabins."

"Sabrina has enough experience to handle *anything*," said Arthur, breezing past her and out the door. "Come on, people! Let's get moving!"

"Oh, no!" moaned a male counselor. "Cabin four."

"Sorry, pal," said another counselor, slapping him on the back.

Before Sabrina could hear any more, Mitch put a comforting hand on her shoulder and steered her toward the door. "Come on, I'll show you the way."

In the lobby Sabrina picked up her duffel bag, which was beginning to feel really heavy, and followed Mitch out the door. They were soon walking by themselves down a forest path. Sabrina had nervous butterflies in her stomach.

"What's the deal with Cabin thirteen?" she asked.

Mitch cleared his throat. "Oh, it's just sort of a camp tradition. With your experience, you won't have any problem. There's a map of this place in the front of your handbook."

Sabrina opened up her thick book and was glad to see the colorful map. Mitch pointed to the

Dining Hall. "Cabins number one through ten are south of here, and all the others are north. You just look for this path and start walking up the hill."

"You follow your nose to the outhouses," said Sabrina.

Mitch laughed. "That's what they say. This place must seem like the sticks compared to those places you worked before."

Sabrina smiled nervously. "Oh, I always feel like I'm starting over with a new camp."

"That's good." Mitch grinned shyly and looked away. "You know, most people with all your experience would be know-it-alls. It's great that you're so natural and friendly."

"Listen, Mitch, I don't know what people are saying about me, but you should treat me just like anybody else. I'm nothing special." Sabrina frowned. "I mean, as far as a camp counselor, I'm nothing special."

"You have confidence," said Mitch. "I like that in a girl. There's Cabin eleven, the first of the upper cabins."

As they walked, he pointed out several small, square cabins, all of which were painted red and had one door and four screened windows. They stopped at a high point on the path, and Mitch pointed out the buildings below them—the Rec Center, the Dining Hall, and the Lodge. In the distance they could see the sparkling river, snaking through the trees.

They reached the red building marked CABIN 13.

He stopped and looked at her with his deep blue eyes.

"There's a lot more to show you," said Mitch. "Do you want to take a walk after dinner?"

"Sure!" chirped Sabrina. Then she frowned, feeling the weight of the thick book in her hands. "But I've got to memorize this handbook by tomorrow. Can I take a rain check?"

"Yeah. You'll probably be busy, getting to know your campers." He gave her a wave and walked off. "See you later."

"Later!" she echoed.

She looked at Cabin 13 and wondered why everybody had acted so weird when it was assigned to her. It looked just like all the other cabins. They said it wasn't haunted, so what was the problem? *It's probably some prank they pull on all the new counselors. . . .*

She traipsed through the old leaves which littered the path and shuffled up to the door. Taking a deep breath, Sabrina pushed the wooden door open. The hinges creaked as if they hadn't seen any oil in a long time, but no ghosts jumped out.

Inside the cabin the furnishings were very sparse. There were exactly five bunks—ten beds in all—and no place to sit down unless you sat on a bottom bunk. The mattresses were bare, and she was glad she had brought her own sheets, blanket, and pillow. Sabrina hit the light switch, and a naked bulb flickered on over her head.

The rookie counselor quickly saw that one rule

had not been obeyed. Initials and names had been carved and written all over the beams and walls. She looked out the back window and saw a small outhouse. A half-moon was cut into the door, in case one couldn't tell what it was from the distant smell.

She yanked the duffel bag off her shoulder and tossed it into a corner. Immediately there came a loud yowl, and a familiar voice cried, "Hey! Watch it!"

Sabrina crept closer and unloosened the drawstring, and a black cat crawled out. "Salem!"

"I thought you'd never unpack!" muttered Salem.

"What are *you* doing here?" asked Sabrina angrily.

The cat looked around at the dismal surroundings. "I should ask you the same thing. This is *worse* than the Middle Ages."

"Yeah, but at least I'm supposed to be here. You're not!"

"You told me summer camp was so great—I had to see for myself. So . . . when are we going home?"

"We're not going home. I'm staying here—don't ask me why—but *you* are going home just as soon as I do the incantation." Sabrina rolled up her sleeves, ready to cast a molecular-transference spell.

"I can't leave you here all by yourself," insisted Salem. "I'll have to look after you—until you come to your senses and decide to leave."

"But animals aren't allowed in the cabins."

"Technically, I'm not an animal," muttered the cat, licking his paw and smoothing his whiskers. "I'm a master warlock, remember. I just had a little bad luck."

"Believe me, the camp director would consider you to be an animal. You'll get me fired!"

"You should be so lucky," grumbled the cat.

Before Sabrina could send the cat back to his litter box, the door banged open, and a stocky little girl entered. She dropped her luggage with a loud bang, and Salem dashed out the door, running right past her.

"Oh, great," snapped the girl. "I'm here for five seconds, and a black cat runs across my path!"

Another girl, wearing thick glasses, stumbled into the cabin. "Is that your cat?" she asked excitedly. "I love cats!"

"Uh, no, he's not my cat," answered Sabrina quickly. "He must be a stray cat who probably . . . lives in the woods."

"Poor thing," said the nerdy girl.

"I hope a bear eats him," said the other girl.

"Me, too," muttered Sabrina. She fumbled in her envelope for her list of campers. "Hi, I'm Sabrina, your counselor."

"Duh," said the first girl. She tossed her sleeping bag onto the top bunk closest to the door. "That's *my* bunk. There's no problem with that, I hope."

"And you would be Attila the Camper," remarked Sabrina.

"Oh, a sense of humor," said the girl. "That's a good thing in this cabin. I'm Rhonda Garwicz."

"Yep," said Sabrina, checking her list, "you're supposed to be in Cabin thirteen."

"Where else?"

"I want a top bunk, too," said the other girl, throwing her gear onto the closest bunk.

"Keep that kleptomaniac away from your stuff," warned Rhonda.

"Kleptomaniac?" asked Sabrina, surprised. "Do you know what that word means?"

"Yeah, somebody who steals your stuff."

The girl with glasses frowned. "I was only caught once. Maybe twice."

There was a sinking feeling in Sabrina's stomach. "What's your name?"

"Karen Litton. With two *T*'s."

Sabrina checked off her name just as a gigantic snake crawled in through the window and dropped at her feet. "Aaggh!" screamed the teenager, leaping back in fright. The other two girls screamed as well.

A peal of laughter sounded outside the window, and Sabrina took a closer look at the snake. It wasn't moving. It was made of rubber.

Rhonda ran toward the door, fists flying. "Patty, you knock that off, or I'll cream your face!"

Sabrina caught the girl and pulled her back. "Hold on there! Who did that?"

A freckle-faced redheaded girl poked her head above the windowsill and grinned. "Gotcha!"

"Patty Henderson," said Karen. "The worst practical joker at Camp Bearclaw."

"You mean, the *best* practical joker!" The little redhead rushed around to the door and strolled in. She instantly threw her gear onto another one of the top bunks. "Can I have my snake back, please?"

"No," said Sabrina, picking up the rubber reptile. "I think I'll keep it."

"That's okay, there's more where that came from." Patty smiled ominously.

A moment later a skinny blond-haired girl walked through the door. Without saying anything, or looking at anyone, she took the next-to-last top bunk. Then she opened up her suitcase, took out a hand-held video game, and began to play. An intense look came over her face.

As beeps and bloops filled the cabin, Sabrina strolled over to the newcomer. "Hi, I'm Sabrina. Do you have a name?"

The girl said absolutely nothing. She never looked up from her game. Sabrina glanced at the other girls, and they all shrugged, as if they didn't know this one.

From the doorway came a voice: "Her name's Alicia, and she got kicked out of another cabin already and put into this one. That's fast work."

A tiny dark-haired girl strode into the room, and she pointed at Karen. "And that girl will try to steal your stuff. And Rhonda is always fighting and being a bully."

"Well, if it isn't Sylvia the Snitch," grumbled

Rhonda. "What would Cabin thirteen be without our little tattletale? If you snitch on me, I'll knock your block off!"

"Hi, Sylvia," said Sabrina glumly. "Welcome aboard."

"And I heard about *you*," claimed the snitch, staring at Sabrina under her long bangs. "They say you're a hotshot counselor, but you must have done something wrong to get this cabin."

Sabrina rolled her eyes. "No kidding. I suppose you're going to take the last of the top bunks?"

"Of course." Sylvia promptly threw her sleeping bag onto the last one. "I deserve it."

Patty, the practical joker, started giggling. "The next girl who comes through that door is not going to be a happy camper."

The door opened again, and a pale girl with pigtails stepped into the rustic cabin. Even though she was small, there was a smoldering intensity about her. She looked around at the girls sitting in the top bunks, and she was *not* a happy camper.

The other girls all looked away from her intense gaze. Even Rhonda, who was twice as big as this girl, looked afraid.

"I want a top bunk," declared the newcomer, dropping her bags with a thud.

"Hi, Jenny," said Sylvia nervously. "I thought you were in reform school."

"They sent me to camp instead. Now who's going to get down?"

"Just a minute," said Sabrina, trying desperately

to get control of the situation. "There are five top bunks and five bottom bunks. If we can't agree on who sleeps where, we'll have to switch off. Why does everyone want a top bunk?"

"Because," said Jenny sternly. She looked around the cabin, and her eyes settled ominously on Karen. "You—you're in my bunk."

"I'm not moving," said Karen.

"This is not good," said Sylvia worriedly. "You know, Jenny pulls the wings off flies, and then she eats them."

"Ewww!" groaned several girls at once.

"Hey, I have an idea—why don't we cut cards for the top bunks?" Everyone turned around to see another girl standing in the doorway. She was tall and gangly and wore a baseball cap. "Or we can roll dice. I've got some candy bars—does anybody want to play me for them? Who has spending money?"

"Hold on!" barked Sabrina. "Who are you?"

"That's Jasmine," said Sylvia. "She got kicked out of the other cabins last year for gambling. She kept taking everybody's spending money."

"*Winning* their spending money," corrected Jasmine. "I'm just good at math, that's all." She reached into her pocket and pulled out a deck of cards. "Who wants to cut first?"

"No, no, no!" groaned Sabrina. "We're not going to gamble over the bunks, and we're not going to fight over them, either. We're going to get along and have *fun!*"

Alicia suddenly burst into tears and pulled her sleeping bag over her head. Then Jenny and Rhonda started yelling at each other, and Patty yelled "Cabin fight!" Within seconds all the girls were screaming and yelling at each other. Pillows and sleeping bags were flying.

"I want that bunk!"

"No, it's *my* bunk!"

"Who says?"

Sabrina thought briefly about turning them all into toads, but that would be the easy way out. Now she understood why Arthur carried around a very large whistle. Since nobody was paying any attention to her, she snapped her fingers, and a magic whistle appeared in her hand. She blew it and it echoed so loud and deep that the rafters seemed to shake. The fighting stopped, and the girls looked sullenly at her.

"Cool!" said Patty. "Can I blow it?"

"No!" snapped Sabrina. Now she remembered what Jill had said in the car, about how Arthur put all the problem campers into one cabin. This was it—Cabin 13! That's why the other counselors had felt sorry for her when she got this assignment. These girls were not regular campers—they were all the troublemakers, the rejects!

"What else can happen?" muttered Sabrina.

There came a knock on the cabin door, and through the screen she saw Jill, standing beside a slouching girl who stared angrily at everybody.

"Here's your last camper," said Jill. "Linda Harrison."

"How come she got a personal escort?" asked Sabrina.

"Because she jumped off the bus and tried to hitchhike home," answered Jill.

"Wow," said Rhonda, obviously impressed. "Houdini Harrison."

"No cabin can hold me," claimed Linda, jutting her jaw proudly.

"Wait a minute," said Sabrina. "Don't tell me this girl is always trying to *escape*? Don't you think I have enough hard cases already?"

"You're the Super Counselor—deal with it." Jill shrugged and turned to go, and Sabrina saw her life flashing before her eyes. She looked around at a mob of giggling little girls, and she knew the truth:

This summer was not going to be fun—it was going to be horrible!

☆

Chapter 4

☆

Jill was already walking down the path, away from Cabin 13. Desperately, Sabrina ran to catch up with her.

"Wait! Jill!" she shouted. "You can't leave me with these girls! Rhonda is a bully, Karen is a kleptomaniac, Patty is a practical joker, and Jenny pulls the wings off flies! Then you've got Alicia, who won't talk; Syliva, who's a snitch; Jasmine, who just wants to gamble; and now Linda, who only wants to escape. These aren't your regular campers!"

Jill looked sympathetic for a moment. "Arthur says, 'There's some good in every child, although you may have to look hard to find it.' Trust me, this will be the *worst* group you'll ever have."

"Great."

Suddenly there came a clamor of screams and

shouts from Cabin 13. The commotion was so loud that it startled the birds in the trees, and a huge flock of them took off, squawking.

"You'd better get back there," said Jill. "Remember, you have two hours of get-acquainted time, and then we eat dinner."

"Get-acquainted time," muttered Sabrina, glancing back at the little red madhouse. A tennis shoe came flying out the window and landed in the bushes. Sabrina wasn't sure, but it looked like one of *her* shoes.

"Bye!" said Jill cheerfully as she sauntered down the path.

As a headache invaded her skull, Sabrina walked slowly back to the cabin. She could still hear screams, shouts, and even a peal of laughter, and she knew she was losing control. She had to show them who was the boss of this cabin! Determined and angry, Sabrina opened the door and walked in.

At once a bucket of ice-cold water fell on her, drenching her and hitting her on the head.

"Gotcha!" cried red-haired Patty, howling with laughter.

Soaking wet, her hair sticking to her face and neck, Sabrina stared at six wildly giggling eleven-year-olds. It was only six because Alicia had her face buried in her video game and Linda was nowhere to be seen.

Sabrina counted slowly to ten, trying not to lose her temper. She wondered whether these girls' parents would mind if she turned them into squirrels.

Shivering, she tried not to let her teeth chatter. "Ah, that's just what I needed—a refreshing shower. Now, where did you get a bucket of water?"

"There's a faucet behind every cabin for brushing teeth," said Sylvia, "and a bucket in the outhouse. Patty did it—she snuck out the window."

"Duh," remarked Rhonda.

They're monsters, and they know their way around the camp better than I do, thought Sabrina. *This is like a horror movie, or a bad dream.* "Where did Linda go?" she asked calmly.

"She ran away," answered Sylvia. "She's always running away."

Sabrina's eyes narrowed as she looked sternly from one camper to another. "I know you're going to find this hard to believe, but I'm actually the *wrong* counselor to mess with."

"What exactly are you going to do to us?" asked the creepy Jenny.

"I have my choice of things to do to you," said Sabrina. "But first I have to get Linda back here. Excuse me."

She stepped outside and shook herself like a large dog. In a twinkling she was dry again, and her honey-blond hair looked better than before. If she hadn't been a witch, she would have broken down and cried right then and there. But Sabrina had hidden resources.

Unfortunately, with a snitch like Sylvia, she

couldn't cast a spell where the campers could see her, and she was afraid to leave them alone. All of them were going to need attention, but first she had to deal with the one who had escaped, Linda. Sabrina felt a measure of sympathy for Linda, because she felt like escaping, too.

She whispered into the breeze,

> "Linda, roam free if you wish.
> But meet us for dinner,
> before the first dish."

The air tingled for a moment, and a chime sounded high in the trees.

Sabrina heard something else strange—Cabin 13 was eerily quiet. There were no mad giggles, shrieks, or screams of pain. She didn't think they were taking naps.

With a sigh Sabrina turned and walked back toward the little red cabin. Even though it sounded perfectly peaceful inside, the teenage witch wrapped herself in a protective spell.

Looking for booby traps, she slowly opened the door. Nothing happened. She heard some happy cooing sounds, and she spotted the girls huddled in a corner, fawning over something on the floor.

When Sabrina stepped closer, she saws that the object of their affection was a certain black cat. They doted on Salem and took turns admiring him and petting his sleek fur.

"Who does he belong to?" asked Sylvia.

Jasmine answered, "I bet he belongs to the director of the camp. Who wants to bet?"

"No, he's wild and lives in the woods," said Rhonda. She pointed to Sabrina. "What's-her-name said so."

"He doesn't look wild to me," countered Patty. "He looks like a lazy cat who lies around all day."

Bingo, thought Sabrina with a smile. She knew she should kick Salem out of the cabin, but his presence was having a calming effect on the wild bunch. Since it was against the rules to have a cat in the cabin, that made it even more cool. As a counselor, she shouldn't break any rules, but "peace and quiet" was a more important rule than "no animals."

"I want him to sleep with me," declared Karen.

"No, me! Me!" insisted all the others, except Alicia, who stared at her handheld game.

Sabrina blew her whistle, instantly quieting them. "Salem—I mean, this cat, who could be named Salem—will only sleep on the bottom bunks. Whoever volunteers to sleep on the bottom bunks will get the cat."

At once the cat lovers instantly agreed to give up their claims to the top bunks, and Sabrina was able to get one girl assigned to each bed, which felt like a major achievement. While the girls were finally getting settled, the teenage witch stepped outside and looked up at the sparkling blue sky.

"Thought-gram to Aunt Hilda and Aunt Zelda," she whispered. "Salem is safe, and he's with me.

The job is a lot harder than I thought. The next time you lie about me, make me only *good,* not wonderful."

Angry shouts echoed from the cabin again, and she hurried back inside to find Rhonda on top of Patty, shaking her by the collar.

"I don't like practical jokes!" fumed Rhonda, whose face was covered in what looked like blood. Sabrina looked closer and saw that it was ketchup.

"Gotcha!" rasped Patty as she was being choked.

Sabrina waded in between them and pulled Rhonda off. It took all of the teenager's strength to get the eleven-year-old to let go, and she hustled her firmly into the corner.

"No more fighting, Rhonda!" ordered the counselor. "Or you'll sleep in the *outhouse.* You think you can't do any worse than Cabin thirteen, but you can!"

"Oh, yeah? How?" scoffed the girl.

"Give me time, and I'll think of something. Now go down to the showers and clean up. We'll meet you at the Dining Hall for dinner."

Rhonda stared angrily at Patty for a moment, then she grabbed a towel from her suitcase and stalked out the door, slamming it behind her.

Sabrina whirled to face Patty, and the red-haired sprite grinned, showing off her new black eye. She didn't even care if she got pummeled, as long as she got her joke in! Patty had already pulled jokes on the toughest girl in the cabin and the counselor. She was on a roll.

"Ketchup packets," she said, holding up a handful of condiments. "Very effective at short range, and you can use them to refill toothpaste tubes."

"You think you're pretty funny," said Sabrina, aiming her finger.

"Of practical jokes,
I begin to tire.
From now on,
all your jokes will backfire."

Unseen chimes sounded in the air.

"Yeah, right," scoffed Patty.

Sabrina hoped that no one would notice that she had just cast a spell. Patty probably wouldn't try another trick right away, and when she did, she would be in for a surprise.

"Can we leave the cabin?" whined Jenny.

Sabrina checked her watch and saw that dinner was to begin soon. "You can go to the Dining Hall or the Lodge, nowhere else. I'll be along in a few minutes. I guess you all know the way."

"Are you kidding?" snorted Patty, leading the charge. "Last one there is a rotten gopher gut!"

While the other campers dashed out the door, Sylvia, Karen, and Alicia hung back. Alicia was busy with her video game, and Karen was sorting through her clothes.

Sabrina looked around for her camp handbook and didn't see it on top of her bed, where she had left it. All her life was mixed up with books, usually magical ones, and now she had lost the most important one. Where had it gone? She had a feeling that Arthur Rimbard wasn't kidding when he told her to memorize that book by morning.

Sabrina started to look under the bunk, but her search was cut short by Sylvia the Snitch.

"Aren't you going to report Linda missing?" asked Sylvia indignantly. "I'll do it for you."

"No," said Sabrina. "Don't say anything. I have a feeling that Linda will show up again."

"Houdini Harrison?" scoffed the camper. "I don't think so."

Tossing her ponytail, Sylvia traipsed out the door, and Karen started after her. Just before the little girl with glasses got out the door, Sabrina got a flash of insight.

"Whoa, Karen!" she called. "I need that book. Please give it back to me."

The little girl blinked at her, trying not to look guilty. "What do you mean? What book?"

"The camp handbook. The one you took off my bed."

"Oh, that?" said Karen with a nervous laugh. "I thought it was a book they put in all the cabins, like they do in hotel rooms. They *want* you to take it."

"They want me to know it by morning," insisted Sabrina. "It probably won't help, but I have to try."

Karen sighed, as if being honest was both difficult and pointless. She crossed to her bunk and dug out the handbook from deep in her luggage. Sheepishly she handed it to Sabrina.

"Thanks. Have you taken anything from any of the other girls?"

"These girls?" asked Karen with horror. She glanced back at the weird Alicia, who was still engrossed in her video game. "No, they're scary."

"That's wise," said Sabrina. "Now, go on to the Dining Hall, and behave yourself."

Karen stopped in the doorway and looked up with concern. "Where's the kitty?"

"Oh, he's around," Sabrina assured her. "Now go on."

Once she was gone, Sabrina had only one more camper to worry about—Alicia, who had yet to say a word to anyone. The counselor sighed and walked over to the gangly girl sitting on her bunk.

"You don't have to talk to me," she began slowly, "but you do have to eat. If you want to wait for me at the Dining Hall, I'll walk in there with you."

Never taking her eyes off her game, Alicia slid out of the bunk and padded out of the room. Sabrina sighed with relief, looked around, and whispered, "Salem? Are you still here?"

A loose floorboard suddenly canted upward, and a familiar head popped out. "Is it safe?" asked the black cat.

"Yes," she whispered. "Hey, listen, thanks for making them be quiet for a few minutes. I really appreciate it."

Salem leaped out of his hiding place and strutted across the room. "You looked as if you needed some help. The kitty act never fails—little girls are putty in my claws. Want me to lead them off a cliff? Maybe some of them can't swim."

"No, just stay out of sight for now," cautioned Sabrina, grabbing her handbook and heading for the door.

"I don't eat field mice," Salem reminded her.

"I know." Pointing, she magicked up a plate of tuna fish. She rolled her eyes. "Here I go, breaking another rule. No animals, no food, no turning the campers into gophers."

"I'll be ready to go home when you are," Salem mumbled with his mouth full.

Sabrina dashed toward the dining room, getting lost only once, when she made a right at the swimming pool instead of a left. She wound up on an overgrown path beside a small stream; a sign carved in wood read BEARCLAW ROCK .5 MILE.

So that was the site of the picturesque fire circle, half a mile away. She wished she had time to explore, but right now she had to hunt down her precious charges. Worse yet, she had to be seen in public with them, and she knew they were unruly and unpredictable.

Sabrina looked around, but Alicia wasn't waiting for her, as planned. These girls were going to make everything hard. With a heavy sigh, Sabrina entered the Dining Hall. None of her campers were in sight, and none of them were in the Lodge, either.

Maybe poison ivy or man-eating plants have gotten them all, she thought happily. Still, she had to start hunting for them.

Other counselors passed by with their well-behaved, well-mannered campers, and they smiled at her in sympathy.

As the Dining Hall filled with kids and their counselors, it seemed even more like a big red barn, packed with wild animals. Sabrina looked in vain for her charges, while trying to appear as if her campers weren't really lost. When she saw the camp director, Arthur Rimbard, she ducked into the kitchen and got in the way of the cooks.

She had clearly made a terrible mistake by letting them go off on their own. She would either have to go to Arthur and beg for help, or she would have to use magic to find them—

"I won't eat no creamed spinach!" shouted a familiar voice. *Rhonda!*

Sabrina turned to see all of her campers following Linda into the Dining Hall. Since Linda was the one who had escaped earlier that day, Sabrina was very glad to see at least one of her desperate spells had worked out. The counselor ran to meet her campers.

"Hi, everyone!" She waved cheerfully. When they ignored her and wandered among the tables, Sabrina fell in beside Linda.

"Thanks for coming back," she whispered. "And for bringing the others."

Linda stared at her. "How did you know I brought the others?"

"Because they respect you," answered Sabrina. "They'll follow you—you're the leader."

"I'm no leader." Linda frowned and stuffed her brown hair under her cap. "And I don't know *why* I came back. I reached the highway—I was all set to go home—but something told me to turn around. The girls were standing by the road, looking for me. It just seemed like we should all come in and eat."

"Very sensible," said Sabrina. "Eating is a good way to end the day."

Linda scowled. "Besides, home is not such a great place."

"I understand," said Sabrina. "My home is a little weird, too. You know, Linda, I'm willing to give you lots of freedom, if you don't cause problems."

"What do you mean by problems?"

"I mean, maybe you escape on your own, but don't take other girls with you."

"We'll see." The escape artist hurried to the rectangular table that Rhonda had found for them. Straggling over one by one, all of her campers managed to find seats at the table. All were present, and they seemed hungry enough to behave themselves.

Sabrina was about to sit down with her cabinmates when Arthur Rimbard rushed up to her. He had a pitcher of red fruit punch in his hand. "What are you doing, Sabrina? You're a table counselor! Didn't you read your assignments?"

"Uh, well, uh . . . I started to." Sabrina's loyal campers began to snicker at her.

"Just get moving," snapped Arthur, hurrying off.

Sabrina turned quickly to Sylvia. "What *is* a table counselor?"

"A glorified waitress," answered Rhonda with a smile.

"You have to make sure every table gets their food," explained Karen. "But you can still boss the kids around."

In the next half hour Sabrina was to learn exactly what a table counselor did. Technically, the campers were supposed to fetch their own big bowls of steaming mashed potatoes, carrots, green beans, and stringy pot roast. Once they got the food on the table, they were supposed to serve themselves family-style.

But most kids would never willingly fetch all those vegetables. Plus they needed pitchers of punch, iced tea, and water, which were safer in the hands of counselors.

For Sabrina, the best part of being a table counselor was going to lots of tables and meeting more of the staff. She almost forgot to eat as she met her fellow counselors and some nice, quiet campers. She looked for Mitch, but Jill was already serving his table of rowdy eleven-year-old boys.

Finally Sabrina decided to sit down and eat. Because of their hunger, her campers were well-behaved, almost like the other girls. Jasmine put some quarters on the table and whispered to Rhonda, but nothing terrible was happening. She stuck her knife and fork into her cold food and began to eat. *If I can make it through this meal alive, maybe I can get through the whole week alive—*

From the corner of her eye, she saw a white missile fly from her table, arc across the aisle, and land at another table. Rhonda gave a whoop of joy and grabbed Jasmine's quarters off the table.

Sabrina was about to ask what they were doing when a pile of green beans flew from the other table and landed on the back of Jenny's neck. The girl froze, and her eyes widened with shock. Before Sabrina could move, Jenny grabbed a handful of carrots and flung them at the other table.

"Food fight!" shouted Patty.

It was no contest. When her rowdy campers jumped into action, they hurled tons of food at the other tables before they could even react. Sabrina started to freeze time, but a wad of mashed beets landed on her cheek, drooling a red streak onto her T-shirt.

Angrily she jumped to her feet and shouted, "Stop it!" They did, but it was too late. Both tables and the floor between them were covered with blobs of congealing food. The enemy campers were covered with muck, and some of them were crying, while her gang was laughing and enjoying themselves. Even quiet Alicia.

Sabrina raised her finger, about to erase the

mess, when she realized that every eye in the huge room was on her. She heard footsteps stomping closer, and she turned to see Arthur Rimbard bearing down on her.

"Counselor, what happened?" demanded the camp director.

Sabrina thought it was pretty clear what had happened, but she answered anyway. "Food fight."

"Duh," said Rhonda to several giggles.

"With your experience, I expected better of you," muttered Arthur with disappointment. "You're supposed to maintain order."

Sabrina thought about telling him how rotten these kids were, but he already knew that. He had assigned them to her. Still it was terrible to be such a failure on her first day of a new job, and the teenager was too mortified to defend herself.

She grabbed a napkin and picked up a glob of mashed potatoes. "We'll start cleaning up."

"Yes!" snapped Arthur. "And no dessert for these campers!"

"How come?" asked Patty indignantly.

"It was all Rhonda's fault," claimed Sylvia. "She was betting Jasmine that she could shoot a glob of mashed potatoes over to that table. *They* were the ones who threw the food back. It's all *their* fault!"

"That's enough!" exploded Arthur. *"We'll"* clean up. Sabrina, get these campers out of here—back to Cabin thirteen."

"Yes, sir!" snapped Sabrina, anxious to get out of there. She was so embarrassed, she might never eat again. She motioned to her campers to stand up. "Come on, let's go."

With hundreds of people staring at them, Sabrina herded her dirty eight out of the Dining Hall. They acted as if it was no big deal to be kicked out of dinner, that it was almost to be expected.

"We didn't even get dessert," grumbled Jasmine.

"Yeah, it's not fair," agreed Patty. "I didn't put chili powder in their food, or anything."

"That other table threw food, too," said Jenny darkly. "They deserve to get in trouble, too."

"That was some shot," bragged Rhonda. She admired her shiny quarters. "And it won me fifty cents."

Sabrina said nothing until they were outside, under a dark blue sky that was deepening into night. She put her hands on her hips and gazed at her charges one by one. They looked so innocent— just children, really. A few of them looked contrite over their behavior, or maybe it was over losing their dessert.

"Would yelling at you do any good?" she asked.

"Probably not," answered Linda. "Everybody yells at us."

"Then I won't," vowed Sabrina. "We're going to go to bed, and the morning will be a new day. A clean slate. If you're good tomorrow, I won't do anything terrible to you."

"Like *you* could," said Jenny with a snide chuckle.

"You'd be surprised," answered Sabrina with a

glint in her eye. In the morning she would march
into Arthur Rimbard's office and tell him he should
put these girls into regular cabins, and give her a
regular group of kids.

"Now *march!* Back to Cabin thirteen. Hup-to!"
Barking like her drill sergeant at Witch Camp,
Sabrina got them lined up and marching toward
the path. She hoped they knew the way, because she
was lost in the encroaching darkness.

Chapter 5

And so the campers pitched their tent by Lake Slimepool on the shores of the old Indian burial ground. They didn't know that this was the same place where the French trappers used to catch frogs so they could eat their frogs' legs. Exactly at midnight the loons made their lonely cries, and a weird mist floated over the dark lake. Something—with no legs—began to crawl out of the slime."

Holding her flashlight under her chin, Jenny looked like a headless ghost floating over her top bunk. Sabrina, Salem, and the other campers were hunkered down in their sleeping bags and blankets, their teeth chattering and their eyes wide with fright. As her flashlight beam cast eerie shadows on the old wooden walls, Jenny's creepy voice filled the cabin.

Jenny paused for effect, and the only sound in the

dark cabin was raspy breathing. "The campers were sleeping peacefully. They didn't know that something was crawling out of the water—seeking revenge. When the giant frog saw the tents, he remembered the trappers who had camped there a hundred years ago. *They* were the ones who had chopped off his legs and basted them in butter."

Jenny grinned, and the flashlight beam made her face glow like a jack-o'-lantern. "So the legless *thing* crawled into the first tent. He wanted revenge, and he wanted his legs back. Quietly he squirmed through the dirt like a giant green worm, and when he got to the first sleeping bag, he saw a scrawny leg sticking out . . . and he *bit* into it!"

"Aaagh!" shrieked a tiny voice. In the darkness it was hard to tell who had screamed.

"With one giant chomp he bit the leg off and was gnawing on it, when—"

A loud knock sounded on the door, and Salem jumped to the floor and scurried under Sabrina's bunk. "Quiet down in there!" shouted the voice of Arthur Rimbard. "Don't you know it's past lights-out? Turn off those flashlights."

"Sorry, Mr. Rimbard!" called Sabrina, embarrassed. "Okay, enough talking. Flashlights out!"

A second later it was dark inside Cabin 13. "That's better," said the camp director. "Good night." They listened to his footsteps crunching away in the darkness.

"Oh, man," complained Jenny, "he ruined my story."

"Don't worry," said Rhonda, "we know how it comes out. The ghost-frog bites off the leg and drags it into the swamp. But when they wake up in the morning, the kid with the wooden leg finds that *his* leg is missing."

"But I know more ghost stories!" protested Jenny.

"This is only our first night," muttered Sabrina. "Save your stories, so we can get into trouble *every* night. Now, all of you, go to sleep!"

Privately she wondered whether sleep was possible after Jenny had entertained them for two hours with gruesome ghost stories. At least the ghost stories had gotten all the girls into bed and settled down, which seemed like a miracle. Even Linda was in her bunk, not roaming around in the woods.

Just as she was dropping off to sleep, she heard beeping and blooping sounds. "Alicia, turn off the game," ordered Sabrina. Moments later it was quiet again in Cabin 13.

Then the giggling began. It started at one end of the cabin and swept through the darkness like a disease. Soon the room was full of eleven-year-old girls snickering into their pillows, trying to keep quiet but not really. It didn't matter what Sabrina did—these girls were determined to mutiny against her.

"Quiet!" rumbled a deep voice under Sabrina's bunk. She knew it was Salem.

"Who said that?" shrieked Karen.

"I am the ghost of Cabin thirteen!" roared Salem. "Now go to sleep, or I'll eat you all!"

The giggling abruptly stopped.

"Oh, I bet Sabrina did that," said Karen with a nervous laugh.

Sabrina said nothing—she just reached down and petted her kitty. It often paid to be nice to your familiar.

Then she heard a wonderful sound, the gentle hum of snoring. It was followed by a chorus of hums and murmurs as the rowdy crew faded into dreamland. After a few minutes the snoring blended in with the crickets; it sounded as if a hundred lumberjack elves were sawing wood in the forest.

My first horrible day, thought Sabrina, *and it is finally over.*

Sometime in the deepest, darkest part of the night, Sabrina was awakened by the sound of a pop and a slobbery *whoosh* of air. "Eeewww!" shrieked a pathetic voice. "Yuck! What happened?"

The counselor opened her eyes and grabbed her flashlight from under her pillow. In the hazy darkness she heard whimpering sounds, and she directed her flashlight beam across the floor to the bunk where Patty was perched. The camper was covered with so much white foam that she looked like a redheaded Santa Claus. In her hand was a can of whipped cream.

Sabrina stifled a chuckle, but two of the other

campers laughed out loud at the sight of Patty covered with dessert topping. Most of the girls were still asleep, and Sabrina didn't want to wake up any more of them.

"What happened?" she whispered.

"I don't know!" wailed Patty. "I barely shook this can of whipped cream, and the top shot off—it squirted all over me!"

"Serves you right," said a voice that sounded like Sylvia's.

Sabrina couldn't agree more, and she tried not to say, "Gotcha!" Instead she asked, "And what were you going to do with that can of whipped cream?"

"Well, uh, I don't kn-know," stammered Patty.

"She was going to put it in somebody's sleeping bag," said Sylvia. "But now it's all over *her!*"

"Quiet down," cautioned Sabrina. "I'm sure Patty would like to keep more people from finding out about this. Patty, go outside and clean up at the faucet. Then go back to bed."

"Okay," said the girl miserably as she grabbed her own flashlight and climbed down from her bunk. "I still can't figure out what happened."

"Bad karma," suggested Karen.

"Everyone, go back to sleep," ordered Sabrina.

It took the girls a few minutes to settle down again, but amazingly they did. Sabrina snuggled under her blanket, thinking that the whipped cream might have been meant for *her.* Putting the whammy on Patty had definitely been a good idea, but she had to stop using magic on these girls.

Sabrina knew from experience that using too much magic could backfire on her. If she wasn't careful, she would end up just like Patty, with whipped cream on her face.

Sabrina closed her eyes and fell instantly back to sleep.

It seemed as if only a second had passed when Sabrina was awakened by a horrible thud, followed by cries, shouts, and crashing noises. She bolted upright and banged her head on the top bunk. With a groan, Sabrina fumbled for her flashlight, but she realized she didn't need it. Golden sunlight filtered through the door and windows—it was dawn at Camp Bearclaw, time for the day's festivities.

The first activity of the day was apparently a brawl between Rhonda and Jasmine. As usual, the bigger girl was on top, pounding the daylights out of Jasmine, who wailed and tried to cover herself. Sabrina instantly flicked a finger and flipped Rhonda off the smaller girl.

The stocky girl landed in a heap and sat up, blinking in amazement at Jasmine. "How did you flip me like that? Who are you, Jackie Chan?"

"I don't know," sniffled Jasmine, grabbing her baseball hat. "But you owe me a dollar!"

At once, Rhonda charged the gangly girl, and they were soon rolling on the floor again.

"That's enough!" yelled Sabrina, wading into the combatants and pulling them apart. "What started this?"

Rhonda sputtered, "She bet me that I couldn't make two burps in ten seconds!"

"Did you make the burps?" asked Sabrina.

"Well, no . . . but she counted too fast. If I had a soda to drink—"

"Pay her," ordered Sabrina. "You were happy to take *her* fifty cents last night and get us all kicked out of dinner. Anybody who is stupid enough to bet Jasmine deserves to lose her money."

"Thank you," said the gangly girl with a big smile. "I'm glad to see that the free-enterprise system is still alive."

Sabrina scowled and looked around the cabin. "Uh-oh, has anybody seen Linda?"

"Houdini Harrison escaped early this morning," answered Sylvia. "No cabin can hold her."

Sabrina sighed. At least Linda hadn't taken any of the other campers with her. The counselor reached into her envelope, pulled out her schedule, and read it in the dim light.

"Okay," she announced, "we're supposed to take a nature walk before breakfast, and we're all going to gather twigs. Then we're going to take the twigs and a bunch of colorful yarn, and make twig animals out of them!"

The cabin erupted in groans. "Oh, no, not *twig animals!*" grumbled Patty. "I thought I gave that up in Brownies."

"Can't we make something useful?" asked Jenny. "How about animals made out of *barbed wire!*

Then we could put them around the cabin to keep burglars away."

"Twig animals just fall apart," said Karen, fluttering her hands. "Gross."

Gritting her teeth, Sabrina pointed slowly at her schedule. "It says right here that everyone in the camp is going to make twig animals, so get busy herding those twigs! Move it, or I'll blow my whistle!"

"Go ahead," said Patty with a sneer. "I've got my swimming earplugs in."

"Hey, what a good idea!" seconded another camper, and soon they were all scrambling in their suitcases for their earplugs.

"Oh," moaned Sabrina, "you're hopeless. This looking for twigs and working with your hands is called *nature!* That's why you came to summer camp. If not, then why are you here?"

"So our parents can have a vacation from us," muttered Rhonda. There were knowing nods all around the cabin.

"Yeah, okay, so there might be other reasons," admitted Sabrina. Looking at all the gloomy faces, she felt gloomy, too. No way was it fair to stick so many troubled kids in the same cabin. If they forgot they were goof-ups for a moment, all they had to do was look around to be reminded.

The teenager gave her best cheerleader impersonation. "We're all here now, so we might as well enjoy it! Come on, taking a walk will be fun!"

Her darling campers were anxious to get dressed

and get out of the cabin. And as soon as they were outside, they split off in separate directions. Sabrina tried to herd them down the same path, but only Sylvia and Jasmine followed her. She had a feeling that Sylvia wanted to spy on her, and Jasmine was kissing up after causing a fistfight this morning and a food fight last night.

The counselor looked back and saw Alicia sitting on a stump, playing her video game. None of the other girls were anywhere to be seen.

"They'll show up for breakfast," said Sylvia cheerfully.

Sabrina shivered. "That's what I'm afraid of. Will I ever be able to get you girls to do anything I want?"

"Sure, we'll gather twigs," offered Jasmine.

"Good." Sabrina pointed toward an overgrown hollow between the trees. There was a promising pile of twigs covered by leafy green vines. "There's some. Let's get them."

Jasmine smiled slyly. "You go get them. That looks like poison ivy to me."

Sabrina looked again, and sure enough the leaves *did* look like the worst bane of summer camp. There was no way that *she* was going to wade into that verdant trap—without protection.

But Sabrina said something entirely different. "That doesn't look like poison ivy to me."

"Well, it *is,*" insisted Jasmine. "I'll bet you it is. Why don't you step in there and find out?"

Sabrina had an idea. "All right, Jasmine, I'll

make a bet with you. I'll walk into those weeds, but if I *don't* get a poison-ivy rash, you have to stop making bets with the other girls."

Jasmine scratched her scrawny chin. "And what do I get if I win? What if you *do* get a rash?"

"You get five dollars," answered Sabrina. "And you get to keep making bets."

"I don't think the counselors are supposed to bet with the campers," said Sylvia with a knowing grin.

Sabrina turned toward the snitch. "Have you ever seen somebody get poison ivy on their tongue? They can barely talk."

"Oh, I don't believe that," answered Sylvia snidely.

"Believe it," Sabrina said, trying to sound threatening.

"Okay," said the counselor, "I'm going to get us enough twigs to make a whole zoo full of animals."

Muttering a protective spell, Sabrina strode bravely into the overgrown hollow. Sure enough, Jasmine had been right—she could tell by the scratchy leaves that it was poison ivy. She'd be itching like crazy if she didn't have a spell to protect her. That was probably how Jasmine won so many bets—she was observant.

Sabrina took off her jacket and filled it with twigs, then she strolled back onto the path, as if nothing was wrong. Jasmine and Sylvia looked suspiciously at her.

"That was easy," said Jasmine. "You're not itchy at all."

"Not a bit," answered Sabrina with a smile. "We'll give it to the end of the day, and if there's no itching and rash, I win. Just to be fair, don't make any bets until we know for sure."

"Um, okay," said Jasmine, sounding as if she was afraid she was being taken, somehow.

Sylvia rubbed her tummy. "I'm hungry. Is it time for breakfast yet?"

Sabrina consulted her watch. "Yes, the Dining Hall is open." She looked around and saw none of her other charges, except for Alicia, who hadn't left her stump and her video game. She waved. "Come on, Alicia!"

The waiflike girl got to her feet and ambled after the others, somehow watching both the path and her game at the same time. Sabrina let Jasmine and Sylvia wander ahead, and she fell back to walk with Alicia.

"That must be an awfully good game," she said conversationally. "I guess it must be way better than real life."

The girl flashed her an angry glare, then went back to her beeps and bloops.

"Do you ever talk at all?" asked Sabrina. There was no response. "I'm just wondering, because I hate to send you home after a week when all you did was play that video game. If that's all you do, there's no reason to come here—you might as well have stayed home."

Alicia snorted a laugh, as if she hadn't been given that option. Sabrina hoped for a moment that she would speak, but she quickly went back to her precious game.

Sabrina pondered her options for a moment. There was a funny thing about handheld video games—they ran off batteries, and batteries ran down. Since Alicia wasn't watching her at all, she casually wiggled her finger, and the beeps got weaker before they died altogether.

The taciturn girl stared at her suddenly quiet machine and slapped it with her hand. Nothing happened.

"What's the matter?" asked Sabrina. "Batteries go dead?"

The girl looked angrily at Sabrina, then swiveled on her heel and started back toward the cabin. Sabrina rushed after her. "Listen, Alicia," she said, "we're almost at the Dining Hall. Can't you worry about that thing *after* we eat breakfast? I'll buy you new batteries in the camp store."

The girl stopped to consider this offer for a moment, and Sabrina hoped that she would accept her token of friendship. But Alicia frowned and strode back toward the cabin, staring worriedly at her dead video game. Sabrina watched the troubled girl, thinking that she would need more than magic to help this one.

"She won't find her new batteries," said a small voice beside her.

Sabrina looked down to see a smug Sylvia. "How do you know that?"

"Because Karen stole them."

The counselor flapped her arms, feeling totally helpless. "But of course! That had to happen. Listen, Sylvia, you know everything. Can you tell me what I'm supposed to do with you crazy kids?"

Sylvia grinned. "Love us?"

Sabrina nodded slowly. "That's a tough order. I'll think about it."

Breakfast was more nerve-racking than dinner because Sabrina wasn't a table counselor at this meal. She had to sit with her campers and watch them eat. Every passing second she worried that they would go berserk and throw food, wrestle on the table, or do something awful. There were only two campers missing, Linda and Jenny. She wasn't so concerned about Linda, but Sabrina was terrified wondering what Jenny could be doing.

Miraculously her campers didn't behave any worse than the kids at some of the other tables. Still, Sabrina was so worried that she hardly ate her breakfast. She kept watching Arthur Rimbard as he made his rounds. He never came to her table, but he glanced her way a few times.

Arthur, there's no avoiding it, thought Sabrina, *you're going to have to talk to me.* She checked her schedule and saw that she had about fifteen minutes after breakfast before she was due in the Recreation Center to teach a class on poisonous snakes. *Poisonous snakes? What do I know about poisonous snakes, except to stay away from them?*

She went over the day's schedule with her campers, hoping that some of them would actually show up where they were supposed to be. As usual, they barely listened to her. From the corner of her eye, Sabrina caught Arthur Rimbard walking out the door.

She jumped to her feet and told her bunkmates, "I'll see you later." Not one of them even looked at her.

With a grim smile Sabrina hurried after the camp director. She caught him as he was striding importantly between the Dining Hall and the Lodge. "Mr. Rimbard, may I talk to you, please?"

He looked impatiently at her. "Arthur. Call me Arthur. What is it, Sabrina?"

She glanced at the campers and counselors heading off to workshops, then pointed toward the Lodge. "Could we talk in your office?"

"Ah, one of *those* talks." He nodded brusquely. "Come on."

A moment later they were ensconced in his tidy office. His desk was piled high with files and handbooks, and there were maps, diplomas, and trophies all over the walls. At first, Sabrina thought that Arthur must be a doctor or something, until she looked closer at his diplomas and saw that he had graduated from archery and lanyard-weaving classes.

"I trust you studied the handbook," said Arthur gruffly. "Should I test you on it?"

"I think I'm getting tested enough already,"

answered Sabrina. "Those campers you put me with—they would be a big test for anybody."

"Not for somebody with your experience," said Arthur confidently. "You're the cream of the crop! That's why I trust you with them."

Sabrina shook her head with exasperation. "I wish people would pretend that I'm *brand-new* at this job. I hate to be blunt, but I don't think it's fair to put all the rejects—"

"Special cases," he corrected her.

"Okay, I don't think all these 'special cases' should be in the same cabin at the same time—not and expect to see it standing the next day. It's not fair for *them* or for *me*."

Arthur stepped toward his tiny window and gazed out on the parking lot and the lush greenery beyond. "If you look out there, Sabrina, you'll see three hundred acres of prime woodland leased from the government. We're the caretakers of this land, and we're also the caretakers of 187 beloved children, not to mention the counselors who often act like children. This is a great responsibility."

Sabrina sighed. "You're not going to change anything, are you?"

"We're all aware that those children are disruptive, especially at night," said Arthur with some sympathy. "By putting them in one cabin, we have one disruptive cabin and nineteen calm ones. Simple arithmetic. But there's a wonderful bright spot in all of this for you."

"There is?" Sabrina asked doubtfully

"Yes, there's always a bright spot." Arthur motioned to the trophies on the wall. "Special groups like yours often do well in our Pride Games, which end every session. The cabins compete against each other in contests such as canoe racing, swimming, tug-of-war, the obstacle course, and pitching horseshoes."

He took an impressive trophy off the shelf and held it out toward Sabrina. "This could be *yours,* Sabrina! Your bunch of girls may be difficult, but they have initiative and drive. They could win it all!"

"Nice trophy," said Sabrina, pushing the relic back at him. "But my sanity is worth more than that."

Suddenly the door banged open, and Jill charged into the office, looking upset. "Arthur, there's a big problem." She pointed at Sabrina. "One of *her* campers was caught stealing William's electric cart!"

Sabrina shrugged. "Let me see, which one could it be? Karen? Linda? Rhonda? *All* of them? And who told you about it? A little girl named Sylvia?"

Jill blinked at her. "Well, yes, that's who told me. It was Linda Harrison, by the way, who got caught."

Arthur shot an angry look at Sabrina. "While you're in here *complaining,* look at what your campers are doing! Now I have to drop a million things, including my first lanyard class, to straighten this out. Come on, let's go."

He stormed out of his office, shaking his head and muttering, "I don't know what's the matter with them. We give them *everything* a camper could want. We hire only the *best* counselors!"

Sabrina cringed, and Jill gave her a smug grin as she followed the camp director out. Clearly, because Sabrina was "Super Counselor," nobody would feel sorry for her.

Now Linda had been caught stealing. That was serious business, and it made Sabrina's stomach churn to think about it. She wasn't worried only for herself and how she was going to survive the summer, but also for these kids.

This was a big job, bigger than Sabrina had expected. She didn't know what to do next—run for it, or stay and try to help the prisoners of Cabin 13.

Chapter 6

The teenage witch sighed and headed out the door, after Arthur and Jill. As she hurried through the Lodge toward the main door, she caught sight of the stuffed bear guarding the entrance. Rearing up on his hind legs with his fearsome teeth hanging out, he looked as if he were laughing at her.

That bear has seen lots of campers and counselors come and go over the years, she thought. *If only he could talk, maybe he could tell me how to survive this place.*

Of course, he *could* talk, if she wanted him to. But the Lodge was crowded, and there wasn't time for that now. Sabrina strolled out the door into the morning sunlight, noting that it was a beautiful day—almost a perfect day to take an electric cart and ride around in the woods.

From the top of the path, Arthur waved impatiently at her. "Come on, Sabrina!"

In a few minutes she found herself in another unfamiliar part of the camp—William's garage and toolshed behind the Recreation Center. Sabrina would be late reporting to her poisonous-snakes class in the Rec Center, but at least she didn't have far to go.

When they entered the dusty garage, the teenager saw Linda Harrison handcuffed to a water pipe. The old handyman, William, was standing guard. "Here she is, Boss!"

"You let that girl go immediately," ordered Arthur. "We're not supposed to use handcuffs on the campers!"

The old handyman smiled. "I've been at this game a long time, and I've learned a few tricks. They're not real handcuffs—I took them off a kid years ago. Look, no key."

He reached for Linda's wrists, and the cuffs sprang open at his touch. The dark-haired girl gawked at him in amazement, shocked that she could have gotten away so easily. She jumped to her feet and started to run out the door, but Sabrina moved in her way.

"No!" snapped Sabrina. "You don't leave me here by myself to take the heat for *you!* You can't run from everything, and this you've got to face. You got caught, so grow up and take your punishment!"

The camper glared at her, but she backed up and sat down where she had been sitting before.

"Now, what happened?" demanded Arthur.

"This is what she was after." William pointed to his small, grimy electric cart. It looked like an old golf cart, except now it was loaded with rakes and shovels instead of golf clubs. An electric cord snaked from the vehicle to a wall outlet, so the batteries must have been charging.

"This has happened before," explained the handyman, "so I put a cutoff switch on the cart. If you don't know where that switch is, you ain't going anywhere. I was coming back from my morning chores, and I heard noises in here. She was trying like the dickens to get it started, and I walked in and caught her red-handed."

"Don't forget *me!*" said a tiny voice. They all whirled around to find Sylvia sitting on a riding lawn mower.

"Yeah, that little girl popped out of nowhere and offered to spread the word." William gave Sylvia a grateful smile, while Linda glared spitefully at the snitch.

"Do we send her home?" asked Jill.

"I hate to send a camper home," said Arthur with a troubled expression. "Then we have to return their money."

"But does she really want to go home?" asked Sabrina, puzzled. "Why did you do it, Linda? Where were you going?"

The tall eleven-year-old shrugged. "It just

seemed like a fast way to get out of here. I don't really want to go home, but I don't want to stay, either."

"If you tell me what you're running away from, I'll keep it away from you," promised Sabrina. "You want to be alone? I can arrange that. You want no structure—I can arrange that. If you want to *sleep* alone, there's always the outhouse."

Despite her determined pout, Linda broke into a smile. William and Sylvia laughed out loud, but Arthur and Jill stared suspiciously at Sabrina.

"This is your responsibility, Counselor. See that it doesn't happen again." Arthur motioned to Jill, and the two camp honchos strode briskly out of the garage.

Both Sabrina and Linda let out sighs, and William just shook his head. "I never liked the whole idea of Cabin thirteen. Seems like they're piling all the wood too near the fire."

"I'm going to escape from here," vowed Linda.

"Listen to me, missy," said William, pointing a gnarled finger at the girl. "You don't have to have an attitude to get your freedom. Look at me! I have freedom to come and go as I please—no set hours, no set duties. I can even take a car and leave the grounds, if I want. But I have all this freedom because I get my work done—you've got to do the same thing. Take care of business, then they won't mind if you run off and play."

He waved toward the door. "Now get out of here."

"Okay," said Linda slowly. Sabrina could tell that she was thinking about what he had said.

Linda and Sylvia headed out the door, and Sabrina paused to look back at the handyman. "Thanks."

He shook his head. "I want you to know that the betting is eight-to-one *against* you that you won't make it until the end of the week."

"Which way is Jasmine betting?"

"Against you. She's offering nine-to-one."

"Figures." Sabrina sighed and wandered outside. Already both Sylvia and Linda had disappeared, which was just as well, because she was ten minutes late to the first class she was supposed to teach. Poisonous snakes. *Why couldn't it be sewing moccasins?*

The teenager shivered as she walked around to the front of the Rec Hall and entered the main doors. Inside there were a number of small classrooms, an auditorium, which was full of screaming kids, and a door marked NATURE EXHIBIT. That was her destination.

She pushed open the door and found herself in a really creepy place. There were stuffed animals all around—weird ones like armadillos and muskrats. On one wall were shelves full of large jars. It almost looked like the pickle section at the grocery store until Sabrina got close enough to see that the jars contained dead snakes, lizards, newts, and other slimy creatures, floating in greenish formaldehyde.

Grimacing, she looked away from the reptiles to see several wooden cases full of dried bugs pinned to white cork boards. All of the bugs had long Latin names under their segmented bodies. Sabrina found a few cases of dried flowers and leaves in the collection, but most of the Nature Exhibit was disgusting.

"Well, it's about time," muttered a small voice, and she turned to see four or five little boys sitting on the floor. This was her audience—the ones who had elected to find out more about poisonous snakes.

"Oh, hi!" chirped Sabrina. "Did you . . . did you talk about anything before I got here?"

"Yeah, why you were so late," answered a boy with braces.

"Is that a rattlesnake?" asked another boy, pointing to a fat snake coiled up in a jar.

"Eewww, who cares what it is?" blurted Sabrina, totally grossed out. "I mean, it's too dead to care."

"What's the difference between a pit viper, like the rattlesnake, and an elapid, like the coral snake?" asked one smug camper.

Sabrina squinted at the boy. "I bet you know. Why don't you tell us all?"

"The viper has erectile fangs, while the elapid has fixed fangs," answered the boy.

One boy turned to the others and scoffed, "This lady doesn't know anything about snakes. Come on, let's find something else to do."

"Wait a minute," said Sabrina quickly. "You would be wrong if you thought that I didn't know anything about snakes. In fact, I happen to be a . . . a snake charmer!"

"Sure," said the boy with a laugh. "And I'm Batman."

"Great, but bats are next week. Besides, who wants to see *dead* snakes?" asked Sabrina, pointing toward the ugly jars on the wall. "No, you boys want to see a *live* snake—the most deadly snake of all—the king cobra."

One of the boys laughed nervously. "Yeah, right, like you've got a king cobra with you."

"It just so happens I do." Sabrina looked around, trying to find someplace she could duck into to work some magic. She spotted the door to what looked like a broom closet.

"Wait here for a moment," she said. "Really, don't leave, or you'll be sorry you missed this."

The teenage witch hustled into the cramped closet and scrunched up against some mops and brooms. Twirling her finger in the air, she poofed herself a colorful reed basket and a flute into her hands. Sabrina felt something wiggling in the bottom of the basket.

When she emerged from the closet a moment later, the boys still looked bored but mildly curious. With a very serious expression, Sabrina put the basket on the floor and sat cross-legged in front of it. Slowly she lifted the ceramic flute to her lips and began to play like an expert.

"There's no snake in there," scoffed one of the boys.

Just as he said that, something began to push the top off the basket—from inside. The ten-year-olds watched, transfixed, barely able to breathe.

"It's a trick," whispered one of them.

Then the lid popped off, and a huge cobra lifted its head a foot above the basket. The boys gasped as the cobra spread its thick hood and turned steely yellow eyes upon them. While Sabrina played, the serpent swayed back and forth, its tongue darting between its deadly fangs. It was hard for Sabrina not to laugh at the terrified expressions on the boys' faces. *This was one nature class they aren't going to complain about.*

"It's not real," rasped a brave camper. He reached a trembling hand toward the dancing cobra, and it whipped around and hissed at him. All of the boys jumped about ten feet in the air. When they came down to earth, they huddled in the corner.

"Okay, okay!" he said, frightened. "It's real!"

Now that she had them in the palm of her hand, it was time for the showstopper. Sabrina set down her flute and reached her arm toward the basket. At once the cobra slithered out of the basket and curled around her arm. When the venomous snake slithered up her shoulders to her neck, the campers stared at her with eyes as big as softballs.

"Any questions?" she asked calmly.

Nothing but silence.

"Okay, I think that's enough snake-charming for one day. Come on, Herbert." As if she were removing her scarf, Sabrina casually unwrapped the cobra from around her neck and dropped it back into the basket.

"I'm a professional," she warned them. "Don't try this at home."

"We won't," promised an awestruck camper.

Five minutes later Sabrina was back in her shorts and T-shirt, strolling along the path to the swimming pool. According to her schedule, now she was supposed to teach canoe safety in the pool, before anybody ventured onto the river. She racked her brain, trying to think what to tell them. *Wear your life vest, don't tip over the canoe, don't lose your paddle, and stay away from the rocks.*

Sabrina decided that she would probably need her bathing suit and her tube of sunblock, so she took a detour and headed up the path toward Cabin 13. She could have used magic to get her swimsuit, but it felt good to be walking in the fresh air. After getting through her first class, feeble hope again sprang in her heart that she could survive her stay at Camp Bearclaw.

As she strolled along the path, Sabrina had a feeling that she wasn't alone, and she looked down to see a familiar cat trotting along beside her.

"If I were still trying to take over the world," said Salem, "I would recruit your girls immediately."

"Are you crazy?" whispered Sabrina. "Get off the path! What if Arthur sees you?"

"I'll cross right in front of him," vowed the black cat. "Couldn't hurt."

Sabrina let her shoulders droop. "Yeah, that's for sure. I've already made a terrible mess of this job, although I had lots of help. Do you still want to go home?"

"Not at all," answered Salem. "I'm beginning to like the great outdoors . . . in small quantities. I've even developed a taste for field mice, although the chase is the real excitement. Our obnoxious campers seem to be busy all day long, playing with string and bits of fabric—I can relate to that. That leaves the cabin all to me, and it's very quiet there during the day."

"You don't want me to quit, do you?" said Sabrina with a grateful smile.

"I always say, 'Never quit—make them throw you out.' But I do think you should have a powerful incantation ready, in case things get out of hand."

"Things have been out of hand since the moment I got here," muttered Sabrina. "I don't think I know enough magic to tame that wild bunch."

"Sure you do," said Salem. "Get creative. Excuse me, I think I see a field mouse."

The cat scampered off into the underbrush, and Sabrina shook her head and kept walking. Since she was alone in the forest, she said aloud, "Thought-gram to Aunt Hilda and Aunt Zelda. I'm just checking in to let you know that we're still alive. And we're still here at Camp Bearclaw, although Salem is having a better time than I am.

"By all rights, I should have a grand case of poison ivy, but I managed to avoid that. Of course, everything else has happened to me. I'm trying to do a good job, but I've got a tough assignment. If you know anything about canoe safety or pit vipers, get back to me. Love, Sabrina."

After sending that message, Sabrina felt a bit better. But she knew she was a long way from being out of the woods.

☆

Chapter 7

☆

Using wits, magic, and her bubbly personality, Sabrina survived the rest of the day. Maybe it was because she was so busy that she hardly had time to worry about losing her job. It was clear that they weren't going to fire her unless she seriously goofed up, because the camp was short-handed. They needed more counselors for basic tasks, such as herding the campers from place to place.

Probably, she mused, if her aunts had been truthful about her work experience, she still would have gotten the job. Then she would be an assistant counselor in a normal cabin, instead of the warden of the madhouse.

After classes in snake-charming, canoeing, twig animals, and archery, Sabrina's body ached all over. Even her fingers ached. She staggered away from the archery field with her forearms feeling tight and stiff from repeatedly drawing back the bowstring. She wasn't sure she could even hold a fork at dinner, which was all she could think about.

What she needed was a shower, fresh clothes, dinner, and a bed—and none of those things were handy. Sabrina stumbled down the path, clutching her schedule and wondering what exhausting activity was next. A calm voice broke into her thoughts and said, "Break time."

She turned around and saw Mitch striding toward her from an adjoining path. He looked sweaty and exhausted, too, but somehow it looked better on him.

"Break time?" asked Sabrina doubtfully. "But I'm only *half*-dead—they could still get some more work out of me."

Mitch chuckled and wiped a sweaty curl of dark hair off his forehead. "It really is break time. We have an hour before dinner, and most of the counselors get as far away from the campers as they can. You know, I never got a chance to show you around the camp like I was supposed to. Is there anyplace you would like me to take you?"

"The showers," said Sabrina wistfully. "I mean, for me . . . alone."

"Well, you know where those are," said Mitch with disappointment. He started walking away. "I guess I'll see you at dinner."

"No, wait!" called Sabrina, catching up with him. "Who wants to take a shower? That's part of the charm of summer camp, smelling like a wart-hog. Where should we go?"

"What haven't you seen?" asked Mitch. "The canoe landing? The compost heap?" His eyes twinkled for a second. "The fire pit at Bearclaw Rock?"

Sabrina smiled as her growling stomach got taken over by delirious butterflies. "The compost heap sounds pretty cool, but I haven't seen Bearclaw Rock yet. Is it far?"

"We can make it," said Mitch, grabbing her hand. "I know a shortcut."

Even though his touch felt warm and friendly, Sabrina thought about pulling her hand away. For one thing, she didn't want to be spotted by Sylvia, who was sure to be lurking somewhere. For another thing, she felt guilty about Harvey. They had discussed the fact that they would be apart this summer, but it still felt weird to be with another boy—although it was easy to make an exception for Mitch.

The path narrowed, and they had to drop hands and walk single-file. Sabrina had to hurry to keep up with the athletic teenager as he dashed from one path to another, climbing higher into the forest. A cool breeze floated across her skin, reminding her that it would soon be night.

If I stayed lost in the woods, wondered Sabrina, *would they come looking for me? Probably. Just to keep a Cabin 13 counselor.*

Mitch glanced back at her with a grin. "Hey, one

of my campers was in your talk on poisonous snakes. I don't know what you did, but he was *raving* about you! I think that will be the high point of his summer, maybe his whole life."

Sabrina gave a nervous laugh. "I don't know much about snakes, but I'm good at presentation."

"He said something about you having a real cobra?" Mitch looked at her curiously.

"Yeah, well, it was really a rubber snake. Luckily, it's sort of dark in that Nature Exhibit, and ten-year-old boys are easy to fool."

"Is this something *I* could do in a talk on snakes?" asked Mitch earnestly.

Sabrina shrugged. "I'll lend you my rubber snake."

"Thanks," said Mitch cheerfully. He slowed down as the trail became even steeper. "This isn't the regular path, but we want to be able to hang out and watch the sunset."

"Sure," squeaked Sabrina, feeling another pang of guilt. *Girl,* she told herself, *if you want to be true to Harvey, you had better turn around and get away from Daniel Boone right now.*

But her feet wouldn't move in the other direction, only upward, toward the handsome Mitch and mysterious Bearclaw Rock. *I deserve to have some fun,* Sabrina told herself. *Who knows if I'll survive the night in Cabin 13?*

"Now that I hear how creative you got in that snake lecture, I know why they call you Super

Counselor." He grinned back at her. "Best of all, I don't have to worry about you anymore."

"Worry about me?" she asked hesitantly.

"Oh, you know, Cabin thirteen and those special campers. Yesterday, I figured you were a goner."

"Me, too."

"I tell you, it's a load off everyone's mind to know that we've got somebody really good minding those kids."

"Right," said Sabrina with a brave smile.

Mitch glanced at the sky. "Come on, the sun is setting."

Her guide sprinted off, and Sabrina struggled to keep up with his long strides. Her aching leg muscles screamed in pain as she climbed the rugged path, and she almost begged him for a chance to rest. *This Bearclaw Rock had better be something special.*

Mitch stopped suddenly and pointed through the trees. "Now you can see it."

Grateful for a chance to catch her breath, Sabrina gazed upward and saw an odd-shaped rock towering over the gently waving trees. Maybe the rock had eroded since it was named, but it didn't look much like a bear's claw. It looked more like a misshapen human foot, and she couldn't help but laugh.

"What's the matter?" asked Mitch.

"Well, I guess it wouldn't be a good idea to call it Camp Bigfoot."

He smiled. "When you see the rock from the front, it looks more like a bearclaw. Come on, we hit the main path just up here, and the walking will be easier. Of course, you probably love to hike in the mountains."

"Every chance I get," she lied cheerfully.

A few minutes later their steep trail joined a level path that had been trod by thousands of young campers over the years. Once again, Mitch and Sabrina could stroll side by side, and she didn't mind at all if he held her hand. Up here, half a mile from the buildings, it really seemed as if they were alone in the woods. Alone in the world.

There was nothing around them but chittering birds, swaying trees, and the endless sky, which was darkening into royal blue. They passed a stump that was crawling with ladybugs, and Sabrina smiled. There was a time when she would have stopped to collect the ladybugs on her clothes, but she wasn't a child anymore. She had a job, responsibilities . . . and two boys on her mind.

One boy was in France, and the other was right here, so close that she could feel the fine hairs on his forearm rubbing against her skin. Mitch smelled of musk, pine, and wood tar; she couldn't remember what Harvey smelled like. Harvey was cuter and funnier, but Mitch was a bona fide hunk. And Mitch was here—alone with her. He was all part of this bizarre experience called summer camp.

Bearclaw Rock loomed ahead of them, and the

massive chunk of granite had to be forty feet tall. At closer range, it did look something like a bearclaw—maybe a melting bearclaw—but what it looked like wasn't important. What was important was that it was remote, away from everything else in the world, except for the cool breeze and the ladybugs.

At the base of Bearclaw Rock was a large, round clearing, which was sunken into the ground to form a natural amphitheater. In the center of the clearing was a blackened fire pit surrounded by a circle of white stones. All around the circle were benches made of logs and rocks, offering primitive seating. Sabrina couldn't imagine what this beautiful place was like when hundreds of campers and counselors were gathered here. She was glad to be here alone with Mitch.

Without saying anything, he grabbed her shoulders. She thought he was going to kiss her, but instead he turned her around and pointed her back toward the camp. Sabrina gasped when she saw the stunning view. The camp itself was hidden by trees, but she could see a pristine valley surrounded by shadowy mountains. A dark-blue river snaked its way through forests and meadows, and the setting sun gave it all a golden glow.

"It's like being at the top of the world," whispered Sabrina. Her tiny voice was swallowed up in the vast silence surrounding Bearclaw Rock. With the camp nowhere in sight, it seemed as if she and Mitch were the only two people on earth.

His strong hands tightened around her shoulders. "I like to think of it that way."

"I guess you bring all the new counselors up here," said Sabrina. She didn't want to spoil the moment, but Mitch could be the camp playboy, for all she knew. He seemed much too nice for that role, but niceness could be deceiving.

She turned to see him frowning, like a hurt little boy. He took his hands away. "It's my favorite place, and I thought you would want to see it. We can go back down."

"No, no," said Sabrina quickly. She grabbed his hands and held them tightly. "Mitch, I'm really glad you brought me up here. So far, Camp Bearclaw has been kind of difficult, even for me. It's nice to get away and relax—with somebody I like."

"You like me?" asked Mitch, sounding pleased.

"What's not to like?" As they gazed into each other's eyes, Sabrina caught her breath. This romance was going too fast, but this wasn't home or high school. This was summer camp—it was almost like being at war. Tomorrow she might be fired, or quit. While the others were betting that she wouldn't last out the week, Mitch was the only one who believed in her.

His hand gently touched her cheek. "I like you, too."

With her heart thumping, Sabrina lifted her chin and gazed into his eyes. In those blue orbs she saw the anxious yet certain knowledge that he was going to kiss her. Just as their lips were so close that she could taste the chocolate he had for lunch, a big, gooey wad landed on her neck.

Giggles punctuated the air, and Sabrina whirled around and glared at the swaying trees.

"What's the matter?" asked Mitch with alarm and disappointment.

Sabrina reached to the back of her neck and came up with a nasty spitball. "We are not alone."

Now Mitch whirled around. "Okay, who's out there? What's going on?"

Patty, Rhonda, Jasmine, and Sylvia poked their heads above one of the log benches, grinning like cats who had caught a flock of birds. Patty was holding a straw, and she was obviously the skillful spitball shooter.

"Oh, Mitch, I'm really glad you brought me up here," cooed Rhonda, mimicking Sabrina.

"I really like you, too," answered Jasmine in a deep voice. The girls giggled wildly.

Sabrina stepped toward them, wiggling her finger. They had no idea how close they were to becoming field mice. Before she could do anything foolish, Mitch turned macho and charged after the girls.

"Get out of here, you punks!" he yelled. "Leave us alone!"

The girls scattered like a herd of goats, scampering over rocks and trails where even Mitch couldn't follow them.

"I have to be going anyway!" shouted Sylvia. "I have to go tell Jill!"

This remark brought another gale of laughter before the odious campers ducked out of sight.

Mitch rubbed his face and gazed down at the ground. "I'm sorry. I wish we could take those rotten kids, bury them up to their necks in the sand, and let the ants have them."

Sabrina sighed. "I think I read in the handbook that you're not allowed to do that."

Mitch put an arm around her waist, but the moment was clearly broken. There was no telling if the pesky spies had gone down to the main camp or were, in fact, still watching them. Sabrina was certain that Sylvia was on her way to tell Jill what she had witnessed at Bearclaw Rock.

"Is there anything going on between you and Jill?" asked Sabrina quietly.

"She thinks so." Mitch gave her an embarrassed shrug. "I made the mistake last summer of being overly friendly to Jill, and now she's expecting more. But she's not my type."

Sabrina looked up and saw that the sky was deepening into a rich hue of purple, and they were without a flashlight. "Come on, it's getting dark. Let's head back for dinner."

"You don't mind?" asked Mitch.

"I mind a lot. We'll go back, but we'll walk slowly."

Sabrina let Mitch go in ahead of her into the Dining Hall, then she braced herself before she walked in. If facing her eight darling campers wasn't bad enough, she could always look forward to facing Jill and Arthur Rimbard. She considered pulling a Linda and trying to escape, but her hunger urged her to find food. Its odor was making her stomach go insane.

Just as she took a deep breath and prepared to walk in, she heard a loud crash. Sabrina walked around the side of the Dining Hall and spotted Arthur Rimbard lumbering through the garbage cans, knocking them over. She thought she saw a fleeting shadow duck into the woods.

"Get out of here! Darn you. I'll put out *poison* for you!" cried Arthur. With disgust he bent down to pick up one of the fallen garbage cans. Gingerly he shoved a bit of garbage back into the can with his foot.

Sabrina slowly approached him. "Mr. Rimbard, is everything all right?"

"Arthur! Call me Arthur!" He took a calming breath and explained, "There was a big black cat going through our garbage cans. I don't know if he's a feral cat, or a pet that somebody left in the woods, or—"

A look of horror came over Arthur's pinched face. "You don't suppose he could belong to some-body *in* the camp?"

"Oh, no!" said Sabrina with a nervous laugh. "Who would bring a pet to summer camp with them?"

"You never know the weird things that these campers will do." He squinted at Sabrina and reconsidered. "Okay, maybe you do know. The point is, I'm getting *rid* of that cat, and whoever brought him here."

With determination Arthur slammed two garbage cans upright and stalked off toward the front of the building. Sabrina looked around at the shadowy forest behind the Dining Hall, and she hoped that Salem had heard Arthur's threat. He had talked about putting poison out, and that was serious.

She wished she could protect Salem, but she was too busy with her own problems to watch out for the familiar. Maybe she should send him home, but she liked having at least one creature she could trust. From now on, they would have to be extra careful around the cabin, too.

Sabrina replaced a lid on a garbage can and walked back toward the entrance. Taking another deep breath, she strode inside the hall, trying to look as if nothing had happened. *Today has been just a wonderful day at summer camp!* At least that was the message she tried to plaster on her foolish face.

It didn't work. The Dining Hall was its usual bedlam, but every eye was still on her as she walked between the tables. They all knew that one of her campers had tried to steal a golf cart, and that her whole cabin had been kicked out of dinner last night. They probably knew that she had kissed

Mitch at Bearclaw Rock and brought her cat with her!

She hurried to her table, trying to avoid looking at the other counselors. To her relief—and horror—all eight of her campers were present, and they looked at her expectantly, as if waiting for her to make the first move. Of course, Alicia didn't look at her—she just kept playing her video game.

Since there were already bowls of food on the table, Sabrina sat down and grabbed a plate. "It's okay," she whispered to her campers. "I'm not going to freak out until after I eat. Then we'll see what happens to you."

"Oh, Mitch," mimicked Rhonda, "I'm really glad you brought me here."

"I like you, too," chirped Jasmine. "Can I feel your muscles?" The other girls laughed uproariously.

Sabrina gave them a steely glare. "I did not say, 'Can I feel your muscles?' And that joke is going to get real old, real fast. By the way, Jasmine, you don't see any poison ivy on me, so you've made your last bet."

"I can always play the Bingo games," said Jasmine.

The counselor looked beseechingly at her campers. "I want to see if we can get through one meal without something terrible happening. Okay?"

The girls were already ignoring her, as usual. As they chattered and argued, they weren't exactly quiet, but they weren't behaving any worse than the campers at the other tables. She looked around for Mitch, but she couldn't see him anywhere. Maybe he was helping out in the kitchen.

There was nothing left to do but eat. Sabrina scooped up a spoonful of baked beans and gulped it down. They were the most wonderful baked beans she had ever tasted. . . .

Suddenly the girls at her table became deathly quiet. They were all staring at her. Sabrina didn't know what was wrong until an entire bowl of Jell-O landed on top of her head. As the lime green gelatin oozed down her neck and under her shirt, she looked up to see Jill's angry, tearful face.

Then she looked over and saw Sylvia, smiling proudly. She had done her job. Everyone in the huge hall was quiet, and they were all staring at Sabrina, wondering what she would do.

The deathly silence was interrupted by a loud cry.

"Food fight!" screamed Patty.

Chapter 8

☆

As food started flying all around Sabrina, Jill burst into tears and stormed out of the Dining Hall. Arthur Rimbard charged across the room, heading straight toward Sabrina.

As anger welled inside her, she slammed her hands on the table and shouted, "Stop it!"

The wildness in her eyes got the attention of her rowdy campers. They stared at her, realizing that a counselor covered in green Jell-O was not to be trifled with.

"Sabrina!" yelled Arthur Rimbard. "What is the meaning of this? Now *you* started a food fight!"

Before she could answer, Sylvia cut in. "Oh, no, it wasn't her! It was *Jill,* after she found out about Sabrina and Mi—"

Sabrina pointed her finger, and Sylvia's mouth clamped tightly shut. "Mmmm-mumble-mmmff!"

she tried to say. The girl with the curly hair gawked helplessly at the adults.

"Lockjaw," explained Sabrina. "I'd better take her to the nurse. Come on, let's go."

At once her campers jumped to their feet. If there was one thing they were good at doing, it was beating a hasty retreat when people got mad at them. Even though it was hard to be efficient while covered with lime gelatin, Sabrina got them marching in a straight line toward the door.

She glanced back at Arthur and saw that he was still in shock. He couldn't believe that his precious Jill had thrown a bowl of food on another counselor. *Oh, well,* thought Sabrina, *he'll have to deal with that. I have my own problems.*

Sabrina looked at her eight problems, walking ahead of her. They exited the Dining Hall talking cheerfully, except for Sylvia, whose mouth was still clamped shut by a spell. As soon as they were outside, Sabrina twirled her finger and broke the spell.

"Hey, hey!" shrieked Sylvia with glee. "I can talk again! I can *talk!*"

"Duh," replied Rhonda. "But that was a good move to get us out of there." The girl looked back at Sabrina and started to laugh, and she was joined by several others.

The teenager supposed she couldn't blame Rhonda for laughing. One counselor dumping food on another counselor had to be the perfect end to a perfect day at summer camp. As bad as dinner was, the worst could still be ahead of her.

What I am going to do with them? wondered Sabrina. *What can I say that will make them behave?*

Salem had told her to prepare an incantation in case things got out of control. *How much farther out of control could they get?* She didn't even want to think about it.

One of the girls slowed down to walk beside her, and Sabrina was surprised to find that it was Linda, the escape artist. The teenage witch was in no mood to make small talk.

"I hope you guys are happy," muttered Sabrina. "You ruined my job, you ruined my love life, and now you ruined my dinner. *Again!* There isn't much more you guys can do to me."

"Hey," protested Linda, "I didn't have anything to do with what happened at Bearclaw Rock. I wasn't there. I keep to myself, and I respect other people's privacy."

"Yeah, you weren't there," said Sabrina. "Sorry I said that. However, you *did* ruin my job."

The girl looked down and kicked a stone. "Yeah, well, we all gotta do what we gotta do. Listen, Sabrina, I still want to say thanks to you. When I got caught this morning, you didn't yell at me, and you tried to understand what was bugging me. I don't think you really know what it's like to be weird."

Sabrina snorted a laugh. "You don't know what weird is. Trust me when I say that I'd be just as happy to escape with you."

"But what about Mitch?" asked Linda. "He's sort of cute."

"Okay," admitted Sabrina, "so there's *one* reason to stay and fifty reasons to leave. I need more reasons than that—I need at least one of you girls to give me a break."

"Okay," said Linda, "I've never been any good at being good, but I'll try for you. I think you're all right."

The counselor wished she could say the same thing about Linda, but she wasn't in a charitable mood. The youngster just nodded and walked off to join the others farther up the path.

When they strolled past the swimming pool, Sabrina looked wistfully at the darkened locker rooms and knew that she couldn't avoid it any longer. She had to take a shower. There's nothing like a shower when you're covered with Jell-O, even for a witch.

"Go on to the cabin," she told her charges. "Please don't destroy it until I get there."

"The showers are probably locked," Linda warned her. "Maybe I can find a way to get you in."

"That's okay, I can manage. Go on!"

All except Linda were already winding their way up the trail to the northern cabins. Their flashlights bobbed between the tree trunks like a swarm of giant fireflies. All the other campers were doing sing-alongs and rehearsing skits after dinner. Not her kids, and they didn't care.

Sabrina shook her head and felt some Jell-O slide down her back. Grimacing, she walked toward the squat brick building and sprung the padlock with a flick of her finger. As she stepped inside the deserted locker room, she snatched a towel and a bar of soap out of thin air. Then her clothes disappeared as she strolled into the shower stall.

Ten minutes later Sabrina felt almost human again as she walked out of the locker room. She was dressed in new clothes, which looked just like her old clothes, minus the Jell-O. Her flashlight beam probed the darkness, but she wasn't walking very fast. Sabrina was really in no hurry to reach Cabin 13.

In the distance she could hear youthful voices singing in the Recreation Hall. Those happy, well-behaved children seemed to be at an entirely different camp from the one she was at. In her camp there were only horrid surprises, giggles, spitballs, thefts, and practical jokes.

"Sabrina!" called a voice. "Is that you?"

She turned to see another flashlight beam bouncing toward her, and it was manned by an earnest and concerned Mitch. "Sabrina! I just heard what happened!" he said with alarm. "Are you all right?"

"Yeah, I'm all right," she answered. "Though I think they ought to put me in charge of food fights. Maybe we could make it a regular activity."

"Well, for you, it *is* a regular activity," said Mitch with a smile. He shined the light in her face, then quickly turned it off. "You don't look too bad."

"I got cleaned up. So where's the champion Jell-O tosser?"

"Jill?" Mitch shook his head in amazement. "I can't believe she did that. Man, what an overreaction."

Sabrina sighed. "Well, she warned me you were taken. I'll listen next time a girl tells me that."

"But I'm not taken!" protested Mitch. "It's all in her imagination."

"You never kissed her?"

He bowed his head. "Okay, I kissed her at the end of last summer."

"Well, it's like this—you need to work it out with her first. When *she* comes and tells me that you're not taken, I'll know you're not taken. You need to talk to Jill."

"If I can find her. I suppose I should go looking for her, but I wanted to find *you* first."

Sabrina waved him away. "Well, you found me. Now go on and find Jill."

"You're something special," Mitch said fondly. He started off, then turned back. "Listen, while I was looking for you, I went by your cabin. They're getting a little rowdy up there."

"What a surprise." She gave him a brave smile. "Now that I'm clean again, I'm ready for them!"

"You can handle it!" he said encouragingly. "Bye!"

"Bye!" She waved, wondering if she would ever be ready for the campers in Cabin 13. With a heavy sigh, Sabrina directed her flashlight off the sidewalk into the woods. A few minutes later she was climbing the path to the upper cabins, but not walking very quickly.

Sabrina felt a familiar presence padding along beside her, and she looked down to see a plump black cat. "Hello, Salem. I guess you got your own dinner tonight."

"I tried," said the cat, "but the raccoons got all the good stuff. Tell me, do these people ever eat anything but beans?"

Sabrina licked her lips. "I shouldn't have thought about dinner." She held out her hand, and a hot dog appeared in her fingers. It was fixed just the way she liked it, with mustard and relish. She ate hungrily as she and the familiar strolled along the path.

"I know you're not a great counselor," said Salem, "but you didn't deserve to have a bowl of green slime dumped on your head."

Sabrina sighed. "That wasn't for being a lousy counselor, which I am. That was because of jealousy, a woman scorned, that sort of thing."

"Oh," said Salem with understanding. "You work fast."

"That's what Jill thought." Sabrina yawned wearily. "Right now, I just want to go to sleep. And there's almost no chance of that."

"Why don't we go check into a hotel?" asked Salem. "And get some room service. We can come back here during the day."

Sabrina frowned at her cat. "You really should go

somewhere else. If you stay here, you've got to be careful to avoid Arthur, the camp director. He has a thing against animals."

Salem nodded. "So he lives in the woods, surrounded by animals."

"I think the stuffed ones are his favorite," she added with a smile. "Stay far, far away from him. I wish I could send us both home."

"We haven't been kicked out yet," replied the cat. "Although I admit, the prospects are looking better and better that we *will* get kicked out."

Then they heard bloodcurdling sounds, including gleeful peals of laughter, loud thumps, and crashes. Sabrina didn't need to see where the noise was coming from—she knew it was Cabin 13. It would always be Cabin 13.

She glanced at Salem, but the chicken cat was already scooting into the woods. Well, what could he do to help her? Plus she couldn't foist these horrible kids on anyone else. That would be a cruel and unusual punishment.

To the other person.

As she cautiously approached the cabin, a curly-haired camper ran toward her. Of course it was Sylvia. "You've got to come!" she shrieked with glee. "There's a really horrible pillow fight going on!"

Something hard crashed into the wall, and it wasn't a pillow. Sabrina could feel the anger rising in her stomach, and the hot dog rising in her throat. "I told them not to destroy the cabin until I got back."

"Well, they didn't listen," said Sylvia indignantly, as if she had nothing to do with it.

Balling her hands into fists, Sabrina stalked toward the cabin. She was about to turn off her flashlight, when the only lightbulb in the cabin broke, plunging it into darkness. That didn't stop the fight at all—in fact, it got louder and more rambunctious.

Sabrina kept her flashlight on, knowing she would need it. She wished she had a whip in her other hand, because it sounded as if the place were being torn apart by wild animals.

She threw open the door, stepped inside, and was engulfed in a blizzard of swirling feathers. In the yellow beam of her flashlight, it looked like an eerie scene out of a winter storm. She could see the girls crashing around in the darkness, laughing and shrieking as they smashed one another with pillows, sleeping bags, and suitcases. As Sylvia reported, it *was* a horrible pillow fight.

Despite her anger, Sabrina tried to remain calm and figure out what she had to do first. Because of the darkness the girls didn't even notice that she had walked in. Or maybe they were just ignoring her, as usual. Although a stray pillow had broken the lightbulb, she knew she had to get some light in here.

Sabrina pointed her finger at the bulb, and it reappeared, shining brighter than ever. The sudden light froze the campers in mid-swing, and they dropped their pillows, sleeping bags, and suitcases and stared at her. All of them were panting, a few were laughing, and Rhonda had a cheerful bloody nose. The cabin was an absolute disaster—a mess beyond belief.

Linda let an empty pillowcase slide out of her hand. "Uh, we're sorry, Sabrina."

"No, we're not!" growled Rhonda proudly.

Sabrina stared the monsters down. "You *will* be sorry if you don't stop this fighting and start cleaning up right now!"

"What if we don't want to?" asked Jenny, leaping down from a top bunk.

Sabrina could feel the blood vessels throbbing in her forehead. "I really suggest that you do what I say."

Patty flopped onto a bunk and whined, "Can't we clean up in the morning?"

"Yeah, the morning!" seconded several other campers.

Linda kicked at a pile of feathers, but that halfhearted attempt only made Sabrina angrier. From somewhere in the mountains came a distant roll of thunder, and Sabrina's eyes blazed at the unruly campers.

"Do you mean that you're *not* going to clean up this mess?" she asked with disbelief.

"In the morning," said Jasmine, flopping onto her bed. Alicia looked down at her video game and smiled.

Thunder rolled closer, and Sabrina lifted her finger. "I'm giving you one last chance."

"Why should we?" scoffed Rhonda. "What's-her-name can't do anything to us."

"Wrong answer," said the witch gravely. Sabrina was so angry that she wasn't thinking—she said the first spell that popped to her mind:

> "From now on, you will obey
> Every little word I say.
> Don't talk back or cause a crime;
> You'll be perfect all the time.
> All of you will think as one;
> You won't have any more *fun!*"

Thunder boomed, and the lightbulb flickered overhead. The eight campers of Cabin 13 suddenly bolted to attention and stared straight ahead. "Yes, Master," they said in unison.

"Oh, my," muttered a voice, and Sabrina glanced down to see Salem at her feet, swishing his tail excitedly. The cat looked up at her, impressed. "Now, *that* is what we call a whammy!"

Sabrina gulped and looked at the android campers, who were standing at attention, staring eerily into space. They were like child mannequins in a department store window, only dressed in dirty rags.

What have I done? she thought in horror.

Chapter 9

☆

☆

It was only seven o'clock in the morning, but Arthur Rimbard was walking around the Dining Hall, nervously straightening tables and chairs. He checked in the kitchen to make sure that the pancakes were being flipped and the powdered milk was being stirred. Some of the campers didn't like powdered milk. That was okay with Arthur, because then they drank less of it.

He went back into the empty hall and stood there, nervously twisting his hands. After what had happened last night, he had to be prepared for anything. Arthur never thought he would see the day when his best counselor would dump food on his worst counselor! In front of the campers!

Jill had returned and was back on the job, although she was mainly working in the office. Nobody had seen Sabrina and her wild bunch since last night. For the hundredth time, Arthur wondered if he could just build a tall electrified fence around Cabin 13 and keep them in there until the session was over on Saturday. He had to admit, Sabrina had been a disappointing failure as a counselor.

Of course, she wasn't the first one to fail to control the denizens of Cabin 13. More than one counselor had run screaming into the night from that bunch. But Arthur had had such high hopes for Sabrina, with all her experience—and what had happened? So far, she had been the *worst* of all the counselors to be assigned to Cabin 13.

A few early-bird campers started drifting into the Dining Hall, with their bleary-eyed counselors not far behind. The counselors went straight to the coffee, and the kids shot toward the sugary breakfast cereals. A new day was dawning, and Arthur could only hope that it would be better than the last one. But it wouldn't be, unless *somebody* got control over Cabin 13.

Arthur Rimbard shivered, because he was afraid that the somebody would have to be *him*.

The camp director got himself a cup of coffee and was just taking a sip when he heard the tromping of feet. He looked up to see a counselor marching her students into the Dining Hall. *Isn't that nice*, thought Arthur. *Such a well-behaved group of campers*. And they looked so sharp in their white T-shirts and shorts, with their faces clean and hair tied neatly back.

That counselor is doing an excellent job, decided Arthur. Her back was toward him as she seated her campers at a table. They all sat down in unison, as if they had been drilled. *Who is that amazing counselor?*

Sabrina turned around and waved. "Hi, Arthur!"

Arthur spit his coffee halfway across the room when he saw who it was. *Sabrina? Are those the girls from Cabin 13?*

He walked over to her table, fearing that it was some kind of optical illusion. But, no, his eyes were not deceiving him—these were the same girls who had disrupted the Dining Hall the last two nights. Now they sat at the table like perfect angels, with their hands folded in front of them.

"Well, hello, campers," said Arthur, not concealing his surprise.

When they said nothing, Sabrina cleared her throat. "Say hello to Mr. Rimbard."

"Hello, Mr. Rimbard," the eight girls repeated in unison.

"I hope we aren't going to have a repeat of what we had the last two days," said Arthur sternly.

"I don't think so," answered Sabrina. "We're under control, aren't we, girls?"

"Yes," they answered in a monotone.

"Hmmm," said Arthur, quite impressed. "Well, this is a very good start to the day. Keep it up, Sabrina."

"No problem," she assured him. "Uh, what's for breakfast?"

"The pancakes look very good this morning," said Arthur.

Sabrina nodded and turned to the absolute worst of them, a girl whom Arthur often saw in his nightmares. "Rhonda," she said, "will you please get pancakes for everybody?"

"Yes, Sabrina," answered the girl. She jumped to her feet and went straight to the kitchen.

"Patty, would you get us our syrup and milk?"

"Yes, Sabrina." The pigtailed imp jumped to her feet and rushed to obey the order.

Arthur was so impressed that he hardly knew what to say. "I guess we've turned the corner, haven't we, Sabrina?"

She nodded slowly. "You might say that. Uh, did Jill ever come back?"

"Yes. In fact, I was going to call both of you to a meeting in my office after lunch."

"I'll be there," promised Sabrina.

"Good. Good." Arthur clapped his hands together. "Carry on!"

He walked away, beaming to himself. *If only this were actually true, that the campers of Cabin 13 are going to behave—it would be like a miracle!*

Arthur glanced worriedly over his shoulder. They were still sitting there, hands folded, not talking. This was a good sign, but it was still too soon to tell. One normal breakfast did not make them a model cabin. He would have to keep his eye on them. Yes, he would.

* * *

After Arthur walked away, Sabrina breathed a sigh of relief. She had no idea why she was so nervous—after all, her campers wouldn't go wild unless she *ordered* them to. But they were creeping her out, the way they were sitting there, hands folded, staring straight ahead. Other kids coming into the Dining Hall were staring at them with puzzled looks on their faces.

"Hey, guys," she whispered to them, "talk a little bit while we're eating. Look like you're having fun."

Linda looked at her and said with a solemn expression, "We cannot have any fun."

"Yeah, well, you can *pretend* to have fun. Do it."

Suddenly they had smiles plastered on their faces, and their heads moved up and down like bobbing-head dolls as they talked. But she could barely listen to the inane words that came out of their mouths:

"How are you?"

"I am fine, thank you. How are you?"

"I am well."

"Do you enjoy camp?"

"I do. Thank you."

"Please pass the syrup."

"It would be my pleasure."

"Thank you."

"You're welcome."

Sabrina could barely stand to hear these lame niceties, but she forced herself to sit through breakfast with them. Now she had the same problem she had before—after breakfast, they would split up and go in different directions. She couldn't watch them, and she wasn't sure they could survive by themselves.

"Listen, you guys," she whispered. At once they stopped talking and eating and just stared intently at her.

Freaky.

"Okay," she said, thinking fast, "maybe you should all do the same activities today."

"We will," they said, nodding in unison.

"And, uh, do what you have to do to survive. I mean, if you're sewing moccasins, try not to stick yourself with a needle. Don't play with poisoned snakes—that sort of thing. Oh, and obey the other counselors."

"Yes, Master," they answered with one voice.

"Call me *Sabrina*," she hissed.

"Yes, Sabrina," they answered, sounding like a Greek chorus.

Sabrina sighed and shook her head. This was bad, and she wasn't sure she could easily reverse the spell she had cast on them last night. Her anger, fear, and desperation had given the obedience spell a lot of power. As Salem had said, she hit them with a real whammy.

On the good side, it was much quieter around the cabin, and her blood pressure wasn't boiling over every few seconds. Sabrina could see the other counselors in the Dining Hall nodding and smiling at her. Everyone was impressed, especially Arthur Rimbard. Perhaps she shouldn't be in such a hurry to reverse the spell.

Then again, these kids would be heading home on Saturday, only a few days away. Although their parents might appreciate the obedience spell even more than Sabrina, she had to return them to normal. It wouldn't be easy to break the spell, but maybe Salem could advise her.

At exactly the same moment the eight creepy campers finished their pancakes, put down their forks, and gazed straight ahead. They were still saying stuff like "I am well, how are you?" but they weren't listening to each other. The hall was filling up, and the other kids were beginning to stare at them.

Sabrina quickly wiped her mouth and whispered, "Okay, let's go."

They pushed back their chairs and stood at the same time. Then they formed a single line with the shortest one, Karen, in the lead and the tallest, Linda, at the rear. Staring straight ahead, they marched out, in perfect step and order. Sabrina hadn't told them to march like that, but she guessed that when people thought alike and did everything alike, they marched alike.

"Hey, look at the dorks!" cried one kid, to much laughter.

"We are well," they replied to the comment.

"Hey," said another, "they're like those robot dudes—the Borg."

"I think they're practicing a skit," suggested a counselor.

Walking behind them, Sabrina nodded quickly to that comment. Luckily, the Borg campers marched fast, and they tromped out of the hall before the other kids could make more fun of them.

When they reached the main path, Linda turned to her with a blank face and asked, "Where do we go?"

"Just keep walking," answered Sabrina. "All the way to the river." She just wanted to keep her column moving, getting them as far away from prying eyes as possible.

They passed the camp bulletin board, which bore a sign reading BEARCLAW NEWS. She saw a big poster for the Talent Show on Thursday night, the evening before the Pride Games on Friday. Until she thought of something better, she would claim that they were rehearsing a skit for the Talent Show. There was no other logical explanation for the worst kids in camp now acting like a bunch of crash dummies.

As they walked, the morning sun broke through the trees, and its warmth cheered Sabrina up. Only a few more days, and the first week would be over. At that point she would make a decision about staying at the camp, but at least she wouldn't leave them short-handed in the middle of a session.

"Sabrina!" called a voice. She turned to see one of the older counselors, Kenny, striding toward her. "Can I ask you something?"

"Sure." Sabrina stopped and waited for the adult. She had seen him in the Dining Hall, and she hoped he wasn't going to ask her why her campers were so weirded out.

"Thanks, Sabrina, I just had a quick question for you," said Kenny. "I saw your campers acting so well-behaved, and I'm really impressed. How do you get them to do something they don't want to do? For example, I'm having a hard time getting my crew to settle down and go to bed."

Sabrina shrugged. "Well, you just think up a magic spell, zap them with it, and tell them that from now on they will obey you."

"That's funny, Sabrina." Kenny laughed and stroked his white mustache. Then he frowned. "Oh, I see what you mean—you use *theatrics* on them. You pretend to zap them, and they think it's funny; so they do what you want!"

"Something like that," agreed Sabrina. She looked around to see where her campers had gone, but she couldn't see them at all. The trail led off into the woods—toward the river!

"What about at dinner, when you—"

"Excuse me, Kenny," said Sabrina in a panic. "Gotta go!"

She ran as fast as she could through the forest, but she forgot how fast her zombie campers could march. The noise of rushing water hurried her along, and she could see the ribbon of blue cutting through the trees. *My gosh, I hope I'm not too late!* thought Sabrina in a panic.

But she *was* too late! She arrived at the riverbank in time to see her charges marching off the dock like a bunch of lemmings! One by one, the campers marched to the end of the dock and plunged into the swirling blue water. They looked as if they were on a pirate ship, walking the plank!

Some of them were already standing in a few feet of water, not possessed of enough sense to save themselves. With a weary sigh, Sabrina waded in and steered the girls back to shore. She was helping Sylvia and Karen out of the water when she heard a snide voice say, "I know what you're doing."

Sabrina whirled in the direction of the voice, and she saw Arthur Rimbard standing on the path, watching her. *How much had he seen?* she worried. *How can I ever explain this to him?*

"I know what you're doing," he repeated sternly.

"Really?" asked Sabrina. "What am I doing?"

Arthur grinned slyly. "You're practicing for the Pride Games. You want to win that trophy, don't you?"

Sabrina laughed with relief. "More than anything. You caught me."

"Great initiative," said Arthur encouragingly. "But don't wear those campers out. They've got three more days to train."

"Three more days," echoed Sabrina with false cheer.

"She told us to go into the water," said Sylvia, who still had a trace of the snitch about her.

Arthur nodded. "Of course she did! You have a great counselor. Keep up the good work!" Whistling cheerfully, Arthur turned on his heel and walked back toward the camp. In a few seconds he was swallowed up by the forest.

Sabrina turned around and saw her eight lobotomized campers, standing there soaking wet, staring into space.

How are they going to survive the rest of the week? Or even the rest of the day?

☆

Chapter 10

☆

Sabrina couldn't believe her eyes. This had to be the most dangerous stunt she had yet seen at Camp Bearclaw! They called it the Tarzan Vine, and it was nothing but a thick rope suspended from a big oak tree. But it stretched over a muddy stream with steep banks on either side. A kid grabbed the rope, jumped off, and soared over the stream like Tarzan, landing safely on the other side.

It looked dangerous. No wonder every camper squealed with excitement as she swung out over the muddy ravine.

In reality, there were six counselors stationed along the route, ready to catch any camper who started to fall. They only swung a few feet off the ground, and landing in thick mud was more fun than risky. Sabrina glanced back at her stone-faced campers at the end of the line. She had to admit, *they* were the only ones she was worried about.

Mitch was the counselor stationed at the bottom of the stream, standing barefoot in about six inches of water. It was his job to retrieve the rope and toss it back to the next camper in line, and he was having more fun than the kids. So far all the campers had made it across the stream but Sabrina's. She kept holding them back, pushing them to the end of the line.

"Come on, Sabrina!" said Mitch, waving to her. "Let your kids go next!"

"But . . . but they have clean clothes on!" protested Sabrina.

"Who cares?" said Mitch with a laugh.

"Yeah, they're a bunch of wusses!" cried a filthy camper who had already gone across.

Sabrina sighed, knowing that she couldn't put it off any longer. She motioned to her strongest girl, Rhonda. "Come on."

Glassy-eyed, the stocky girl walked forward and grabbed the rope. "Jump on, and put your feet here," said Sabrina, pointing to a knot at the bottom of the rope. Since another counselor was standing right beside her and they had already sent about fifty kids across on the Tarzan Vine, she couldn't give the directions she wanted, such as "Don't fall off."

"Go!" shouted Mitch.

"Jump!" said Sabrina.

Rhonda jumped all right—after letting go of the

rope. She rolled down the bank like a sack of potatoes and crashed into Mitch, knocking his feet out from under him. The two of them collapsed into mud.

Everyone laughed, except for Mitch, Sabrina, and the mindless campers. "What dorks!" yelled a kid on the other side.

Mitch got up and tried to wipe off the mud, while Rhonda simply stood there, covered with muck. She didn't move until Mitch said, "Go on with the others." But Rhonda climbed the bank and joined the other campers who remained with Sabrina.

"What's the matter with you?" a ten-year-old yelled at Rhonda. "You act like a robot!"

Sabrina quickly ushered Linda to the front of the line, and Mitch threw the rope back to her. "Let's see if we can do better this time!" he said.

"Okay, Linda, hold on to this, and don't let go," ordered Sabrina. The tall girl gripped the rope as if it were a life preserver. "Now jump!"

Linda jumped, and she held on tightly. For a moment Sabrina thought that it would be a successful swing over the ravine. But Linda swung to the other side of the stream and . . . she didn't let go! She swung back and forth over the ravine like a pendulum, never letting go. Even when Mitch finally stopped her, she wouldn't let go of the rope.

Sabrina shook her head. Because her zombies couldn't think for themselves, she had to be totally specific when she gave them directions.

"Come on," said Mitch with exasperation as he

tried to pull the girl off the rope. "What's the matter with you? The ride's over."

"Let go!" ordered Sabrina.

Linda suddenly let go and collapsed right on top of Mitch, plowing him back into the mud.

"Okay!" shouted Sabrina quickly. "It's lunchtime. Come on, girls!" Before anything else could happen, she escorted her robotic campers away from the Tarzan Vine. She glanced over her shoulder and saw Linda trudging after them.

"What nerds!" shouted a camper, and the others all laughed.

Great, thought the teenage witch. *My campers have gone from being the camp goof-offs to being the camp nerds.*

She turned back to see Mitch looking strangely at her, wondering what was going on. At this point he had to believe that she was the flakiest of the flakes. Look at how she had taken eight fun-loving little girls and turned them into clumsy mannequins. He must think she was awfully weird.

If you only knew, thought Sabrina miserably.

The denizens of Cabin 13 sat in the corner of the Dining Hall and ate lunch quickly, before most of the other campers and counselors could even file into the room. When it began to get crowded, she marched them out the back, through the kitchen.

As they tromped past the garbage cans, a certain black cat leaped on top of a can, startling Sabrina.

"Oh, it's only *you*," muttered Sabrina. "I thought you were a skunk."

"A few more days here, and I'll smell like one," said Salem, cocking his head. "And how are the Stepford Campers?"

Sabrina frowned. "Mindless, clumsy, and creepy. Listen, Salem, I have a meeting in the director's office—could you follow them back to the cabin? Just keep them there until I get back."

"They can't even walk to the cabin by themselves?" asked Salem.

"Sure, they can *walk* there, but what then? Please, keep an eye on them, will you? And don't use them to try to take over the world."

"Drat," grumbled Salem. "You know me too well."

"Girls, you obey Salem," ordered Sabrina. "I'll be back as soon as I can."

Sabrina rushed back into the Dining Hall, leaving Salem alone with eight glassy-eyed girls.

"Okay," said Salem, "repeat after me. 'Yes, Master, we will do your bidding.'"

"Yes, Master," they intoned, "we will do your bidding."

"That's a good start," said the cat, swishing his tail happily.

Sabrina paced in front of the stuffed bear in the Lodge, waiting for Arthur and Jill to show up for their meeting. She wasn't nervous about the meeting—she was nervous about leaving her brainless campers alone, even with Salem to watch them. What had started out as a solution to her problems had now made her more fretful than ever.

She looked up at the bear towering over her and sighed. "You've got it easy, Henry. Everybody loves you, and you don't have to do anything but stand there. They might junk you someday, but they can't fire you."

"Talking to stuffed animals, are we?" asked a feminine voice.

Sabrina turned to see Jill walking through the door. The dark-haired counselor still looked mad, but at least she didn't have any food in her hands.

"Hi," said Sabrina. "I get tired of talking to myself, so I thought I would try the bear. He doesn't say much, but he never criticizes, either."

Jill crossed her arms and looked thoughtful. "I know what you mean—I've been talking to myself a lot, too."

There was a long pause, then both girls blurted, "You can have Mitch!"

They laughed and bowed their heads. "At last we're thinking alike," said Sabrina.

"Mitch is not mine to have," answered Jill quietly. "I wish that were different, but he likes softer girls, like you."

"Mitch and I would never work out," admitted the teenage witch, "because I kind of already have a boyfriend. If I were in my right mind, I don't know if I would've gone up to Bearclaw Rock with Mitch. But those girls in my cabin have got me totally distracted."

"I saw them today, and they looked like perfect angels," said Jill suspiciously.

"Appearances can be deceiving."

"Oh, you think they're up to something?"

"If you had those girls, and they were perfect angels, would you be worried?"

"Petrified," admitted Jill with a slight smile.

Just then, Arthur Rimbard walked into the Lodge and spotted his two counselors standing in front of the bear. "Ah, here you are." He checked his watch. "And you're both early. Excellent!"

"Hi, Arthur," said Sabrina. "We've pretty much worked it all out."

He turned to Jill. "Did you apologize?"

"No, not yet." She took a deep breath and said quickly, "Sabrina, I'm sorry I dumped Jell-O on you."

"It wasn't all bad," answered the teen. "It forced me to take a shower."

Arthur clapped his hands. "Then everything is settled! Now that you two have made up, I want you to be fierce competitors in the Pride Games. I'm expecting a lot from both of your cabins."

Sabrina frowned. "Um, Arthur, is it possible for a cabin to, like, not play in the games?"

Both Arthur and Jill gawked at her as if she had suggested something horrifying. "In the history of Camp Bearclaw," said Arthur gravely, "there has never been a cabin that refused to participate in the Pride Games. Maybe if all your campers were in the hospital—"

"There's a good chance of that," muttered Sabrina.

"Pardon me?"

"Never mind," said the counselor with forced cheer. "They'll be there, playing in the games."

Arthur grinned. "Excellent. Let's not have any more food fights, runaways, or robberies. All we want is that good old Camp Bearclaw spirit!"

"Rah-rah!" answered Sabrina, punching her fist into the air.

"You two are dismissed." With a curt nod, Arthur hurried into his office.

Jill gave Sabrina a sidelong glance. "It probably won't do me any good, but did you mean what you said about Mitch?"

"I'm afraid so," answered Sabrina.

Jill patted her on the shoulder. "You're weird, but I almost like you. See you later."

"Bye."

Sabrina followed the conceited counselor out the door, then she hurried down the path toward Cabin 13. She was supposed to be in the Recreation Center, teaching a class on knot-tying, but she was already tied in knots. Even if she *knew* something about tying knots, she couldn't teach it with so much on her mind.

She knew something was wrong when she approached the cabin and saw Jenny, Alicia, and Jasmine crawling around in the bushes on their hands and knees.

"What are you doing?" asked Sabrina.

Jenny looked up with her creepy blue eyes. "Catching field mice for the master."

"Stop and go inside," ordered Sabrina. She charged into the cabin and was not all that surprised by the sight she found. Salem was sitting on a stack of pillows, and two girls were giving his claws a manicure. Two more girls were brushing his sleek black fur, and Patty was tying a pink bow on his collar.

Sabrina crossed her arms and demanded, "What are you doing?"

"Getting a makeover," answered the cat smugly. "Isn't cat grooming one of the activities here?"

"No."

"Well, it should be."

There came a knock on the door, and Sabrina jumped about six feet. "Hide!" she told Salem.

At once all of the girls stopped what they were doing and tried to roll under their bunks or hide behind their suitcases.

"No, not *you!*" hissed Sabrina. "The cat!"

"Is everything all right in there?" called a voice. It sounded like Mitch.

"Oh, sure!" answered Sabrina nervously. At last her silly cat got the message and scooted under a bunk. "Come in!"

The door swung open, but Mitch only stuck his head in. "No, I'd better stand out here. No boys in the girls' cabins, and all that."

"Oh, right," said Sabrina. "We wouldn't want to break a rule."

The young man looked puzzled at the eight stone-face campers. "Am I interrupting something?"

"No, no!" Sabrina assured him. "What can I do for you?"

"Well, I saw you walking up the path, and I remembered I was giving a nature talk this afternoon. I wondered if I could borrow your rubber snake?"

Sabrina laughed with relief. "Oh, that! Sure, it's right here." She rushed to her duffel bag and retrieved the rubber snake she had taken from Patty on the first day. That fateful Saturday seemed like weeks ago, although it had only been a couple of days.

"Thanks," said Mitch, taking the snake. He still looked puzzled. "Your campers are all supposed to be at classes and activities, not hanging out in the cabin."

"Well, we're, uh . . . practicing our skit."

Mitch smiled. "Oh, I see. It's secret, huh?"

"Yeah. A big secret."

"Okay," said Mitch, backing away from the door. "Thanks for the snake. Say, do you want to take a walk after dinner?"

"No, I'm sorry," answered Sabrina. "I think I'm going to be busy."

Mitch looked disappointed. "Okay, but don't let Arthur catch you hanging out in your cabin during the day. You're only allowed to do that when it's raining."

"Raining?" echoed Sabrina thoughtfully. "Thanks for the tip."

Mitch shook his head puzzledly as Sabrina slammed the door shut. From the window, she watched him walk down the path, then she looked up at the beautiful blue sky.

"We can fix that," she said to herself.

For the next few days it rained continuously at Camp Bearclaw. It was a surprise storm which took the camp director and the weather forecasters by surprise. Hour after hour Sabrina and Salem sat in the doorway and watched the rain pour down. Behind them, eight girls stood at attention like tin soldiers, staring eerily into space.

"That is some storm you whipped up," said Salem with admiration.

Sabrina smiled. "I learned that trick from Aunt Hilda. Nobody is better at whipping up a storm than her." Her grin turned into a frown. "But I know it's not right. Not only am I depriving my campers from having fun, I'm depriving *all* the campers from having fun."

"They're sewing moccasins in the Rec Center,"

said Salem. "By now everybody has four or five pairs."

"I know. I should put an end to it, but I don't know what to do with *them.*" Sabrina pointed to the living statues behind her. "If I remove the spell, things could get worse."

"Let's figure this out," suggested Salem. "Tonight we have the Talent Show, and tomorrow these big games everyone has been talking about."

"That's right. And after the games on Friday, we have the candlelight ceremony at Bearclaw Rock. That's when Arthur hands out the trophies, and we all say good-bye. On Saturday these campers will be gone, and a new batch arrives."

"Hallelujah," muttered Salem. "I'll be ready to go home. We *are* going home, aren't we?"

"I guess so," said Sabrina, tossing a pebble into the huge puddle outside the door. She hadn't decided for sure whether to quit on Saturday, but she didn't know how she could stay. She was a fraud, not a real counselor at all. It was better for Arthur, Mitch, and everyone else if she left.

The rain kept battering the sodden ground and the dripping pine trees. The gray skies matched her mood.

"I hate to admit it," said Salem, "but you can't leave your lovely campers like this."

"No," answered Sabrina, glancing back at her somber charges. They looked like a row of mannequins that had been left outside for too long. "I suppose if I change them back and turn off the rain, we can all enjoy the Talent Show tonight."

"I doubt if hearing these children sing and act will be enjoyable," remarked Salem. "But *you* can go."

"Thanks." Sabrina sighed and rolled up her sleeves. "All right, let's get things back to normal."

"Remember to concentrate," warned Salem. "That was a powerful spell you put on them."

"Well, if I did it, I should be able to undo it." Looking determined, Sabrina pointed her finger at her comatose cabinmates and said aloud:

"I made you obey me;
Now I know that was wrong.
Please go back to normal,
And we'll all get along."

A low roll of thunder sounded outside, but it might have been just the rain. Sabrina looked expectantly at her kids. Jenny's face twitched a little, but that was the only movement any of them made. They remained standing at attention like a bunch of statues, their faces molded in stone.

"Oh, no!" gasped Sabrina. "It didn't work!"

"I told you it wouldn't be easy to break it," said Salem. "Witches are always more powerful when they're really angry, and you were furious that night."

"But I've got to get them back to normal!"

insisted Sabrina. "There's the Talent Show and the Pride Games, then they're supposed to go home on Saturday!"

"Calm down, you've got some time. For one thing, you're spreading your magic too thin by making all this rain, too. Why don't you kill the rain?"

"Okay, kill the rain," said Sabrina, trying to be calm. She snapped her fingers as she had seen Aunt Hilda do a hundred times, and the rain stopped— it was like a giant faucet had been turned off. Moisture continued to drip from the roof and the rain pipes, but the gray skies were already starting to clear.

As a beam of golden light sliced through the treetops, Sabrina heard a camper in another cabin whoop for joy.

"Not bad," offered Salem.

"Okay, we're almost back to normal. Now for the wild bunch." Sabrina wiggled all ten of her fingers at the young zombies and said:

> "You campers used to cause a riot,
> But now you're way too quiet.
> The obedience spell is done;
> So go out and have some fun!"

Patty gave a little snort of laughter, then her face went back to being a blank. None of the rest of them even moved.

Sabrina looked worriedly at Salem. "What do I need to do?"

"Get a rhyming dictionary," suggested the cat. "You've got a lot of spells to go through. The problem is, you'll have to be as desperate to get them *out* of it as you were to get them *into* it."

Suddenly the fur on Salem's back stiffened, and he darted to the back of the cabin. Sabrina looked up to see Arthur Rimbard striding along the path.

"All right, everybody! Get out of those cabins!" shouted the director. "We're going to the Rec Center to rehearse our skits. The Talent Show goes on as planned!"

With a broad smile he waved to Sabrina. "Isn't it great that the rain has stopped? I'll see you and your perfect campers in the Rec Center!"

"See you!" called Sabrina, trying to sound cheerful. "We'll be right there."

She closed the door and slumped against it, looking at her eight frozen campers. *They can barely walk! What kind of talent skit could they possibly do?*

"I'm in trouble," she muttered to herself.

"What are they supposed to be?" asked a boy camper, staring at the denizens of Cabin 13. As usual, the eight silent campers were standing perfectly still and gazing into thin air.

"They're supposed to be a tableaux," Sabrina answered.

"A table?" asked the kid. "They don't look like a table."

"No," whispered Sabrina. "A *tableaux* is a bunch of people who stand around and pose, like they're a famous painting, or an event from history."

She didn't want to speak too loudly, because they were standing backstage at the Rec Center and the Talent Show was in progress. Onstage the campers from Cabin 12 were twirling Hula-Hoops while singing "Row, Row, Row Your Boat." That only counted as a talent at summer camp, but the audience laughed and applauded as if they enjoyed it.

"Well, they're doing a good job of standing around," said the kid.

"Thanks," muttered Sabrina. "I trained them myself."

Nervously twisting her hands, she turned back to look at the stage. So far they had seen some ancient skits with jokes from the Stone Age, plus a lot of off-key singing and clumsy dancing. After all that, she hoped the audience wouldn't mind a group of campers who did nothing but stand still.

Suddenly the applause got louder, and the hoop-twirling singers were taking their bows.

"Let's hear it for the campers from Cabin twelve!" announced Arthur, braying into the microphone. His voice boomed over the loudspeaker, just the way the hyper camp director liked to hear himself.

Several girls rushed past Sabrina with their Hula-

Hoops, and she looked nervously at her own campers. Of course, they weren't nervous at all. A bomb could have exploded underneath them, and they wouldn't get nervous.

"All right," said Arthur, studying his list. "Next up are the girls from Cabin 13, directed by their counselor, Sabrina Spellman. They will be doing a tableaux depicting George Washington's crossing of the Delaware."

"Dim the lights!" Sabrina shouted to Arthur.

Arthur motioned to the back of the hall, and the stage lights went down to near darkness.

Sabrina clapped her hands. "Okay, girls, let's go!"

Exactly as she had trained them, her campers picked up an old canoe and some oars and carried them onto the stage. Linda, the tallest one, was wearing a white wig and a three-cornered hat. The other girls were wearing makeshift costumes that looked something like the Revolutionary War.

Shuffling through the darkness, they took their places. When they stopped moving, Sabrina waved to Arthur, and he waved toward the back of the hall.

When the lights blinked on again, eight girls were squeezed into the canoe. Most of them were supposed to be rowing, and their oars were frozen in midair. Linda stood in the bow, gazing bravely toward the shore. None of them were moving a muscle.

From the audience came a few twitters of laughter when it became clear that this bizarre scene was Cabin 13's act. But after a few seconds passed, the laughter turned to amazed oohs and ahs, because the girls stood so perfectly still that they *did* look like a painting. When two minutes went by—and still not one of them moved—loud applause broke out in the Recreation Center.

Arthur Rimbard walked over to her and whispered, "Very impressive. I've never seen anything like this. How long can they stay that way?"

Sabrina shrugged. "How long have we got?"

Arthur checked his watch. "I'll give you another minute. I think they're a shoo-in to win the Talent Show award."

"Cool!"

The director shook his head in amazement. "You have really turned those kids around. I've never seen anything like it."

"Thanks." Sabrina smiled, but only for a moment. They had survived the Talent Show, but the Pride Games that took place tomorrow would be a whole different story.

More than ever, she had to find a way to reverse that spell!

☆

Chapter 11

☆

"Campers and counselors!" bellowed Arthur into his megaphone. "Welcome to the opening of the Camp Bearclaw Pride Games!"

He hoisted an impressive trophy over his head and waved it around. "This trophy will be presented to the cabin who compiles the greatest number of points in all of our camp competitions. Our first event is the Obstacle Course Race. Good luck to all of you!"

Sabrina glanced at her zombie campers and knew she would need lots of luck to get through today and tomorrow. All last night, she and Salem had tried a dozen different spells and incantations to change them back to normal, but nothing had worked.

They were so desperate that they had even tried to contact Aunt Zelda and Aunt Hilda. But the fun-loving witches were not home—or even in the Earthly Realm. They must have picked Sabrina's absence as a good time to go on vacation in the Other Realm. While the mouse was away, the cats would play.

She and her cabinmates were gathered on the field of play with the rest of the campers and counselors, and there was nowhere to hide. Stretching in front of them was an obstacle course that looked like a cross between a playground and a steeplechase. There were walls to climb, ditches to jump, obstacles to crawl under, tires to jog through, and a rope swing at the end.

Sabrina thought about telling her kids to pretend that they were all injured, but she didn't think anyone would believe that. It was too bad, too. If her campers were their normally energetic selves, they could make quick work of this course.

"Cabin 1 get ready!" announced Arthur. "The way we judge this is simple. Every camper from the cabin runs through the obstacle course, and we time how long it takes for the *last* one to finish. We give three points to the cabin whose slowest runner is the fastest, and two to the second-place cabin, and one to the third-place cabin."

William, the old handyman, sidled up to Sabrina. "Good luck," he told her.

"Hi," she said nervously. "We'll need it."

"I've got five dollars riding on your cabin," said the old man with a smile.

"I hope you can afford to lose it."

"I can. I won *ten* dollars by betting on your cabin

to win the Talent Show." He winked and stepped back into the crowd.

"Timekeepers, take your places," said Arthur. Armed with stopwatches, Mitch and several other counselors took positions at the finish line of the obstacle course. Mitch looked at Sabrina and waved. He was probably another one who expected her cabin to win.

Arthur lifted a starter's pistol. "Cabin 1, on your marks."

Nine excited little boys lined up to run the course. There was a lot of pressure on these kids, but they seemed eager to prove themselves. Her campers looked as if they were still in tableaux mode.

"Get ready, get set, go!" called Arthur, shooting his pistol at the same time.

The boys from Cabin 1 dashed off, and Sabrina had to smile at their exuberance. The first wall was made of wood and was about four feet high. A lot of the kids vaulted easily over it, but the smaller campers had to scramble like mad to climb it.

Next they were supposed to leap over a ditch filled with muddy water, and most of them managed that feat all right. One fell in, and one stumbled on the other side. Then they hit the tires, which were laid out flat on the ground so that the contestants had to put their feet in the holes as they ran through. This was much harder, and only one camper from Cabin 1 got through the tires without falling down.

After that they had to crawl on their bellies under

a net that hung from a wooden frame about a foot off the ground. This was slow going, although one of the boys got creative and rolled instead of crawled. His cabinmates copied him, and soon all of them were rolling.

Sabrina turned to her campers and whispered, "Watch what they're doing!"

"Yes, Sabrina," they answered in unison.

Sabrina shook her head helplessly, then turned and watched the finish of the race. The boys caught ropes in their hands and swung over another ditch full of water, then they staggered across the finish line. As the last one slumped to his knees, panting, the counselors punched their stopwatches. They compared numbers and wrote down the times.

And so it went, with the races looking awfully close to Sabrina. She kept telling her comatose campers to watch what the others were doing—and do it—but she didn't know how much was getting through to them.

Finally Arthur announced those fateful words: "Next up—Cabin thirteen!"

A hush came over the crowd. After acting like juvenile delinquents, then like robots, then winning the Talent Show, the girls of Cabin 13 were infamous. Everyone wanted to know how they were going to do in the Pride Games. Everyone except Sabrina—she just wanted to run and hide.

When they didn't move, she pushed them. "Get to the starting line. Do what the others did!"

"It's the dorks," said one camper, and his friends laughed.

"On your marks. Get ready, get set, go!"

The gun popped, and Linda, Rhonda, Patty, Jenny, Jasmine, Alicia, Karen, and Sylvia ran toward the first obstacle, the wall. It was a promising start—at least they didn't stumble.

But when they reached the wall, none of them vaulted over as the others had done. Instead they fumbled and flailed like clumsy babies. It seemed to take forever for even one of them to make it over, and all of them landed like bricks on the other side. Several kids in the audience laughed out loud.

When they reached the ditch filled with water, her pathetic campers didn't bother to jump at all. They just splashed through the muck, falling and getting stuck. Now the other campers were roaring with laughter. It got even worse when they hit the tires spread across the ground. They stumbled, staggered, and tumbled head over heels on the rubber obstacles.

Even the counselors were laughing now, and Sabrina covered her eyes with her hands. She watched through the cracks between her fingers, as if this were a scary horror movie. Her girls were doing just as the other campers had done, but they were only copying the ones who had slipped or fallen!

When they got to the nets, they crawled on their bellies like a herd of earthworms. They went so slowly that the other campers were hooting and hollering at them. When they got to the ropes, they were hopeless as they bumbled their way into the water.

"I hope your stopwatch has an hour hand!" one camper shouted at the timekeepers.

Arthur, Mitch, Jill, William, Kenny, and dozens of staff members looked at Sabrina, wondering what was going on. She shrugged and smiled helplessly. Using magic now wouldn't help. Finally they did finish the obstacle race, but Sabrina was sure it had to be the slowest time on record.

Mitch brought the results to Arthur, and he bellowed into his megaphone, "We are pleased to announce that Cabin eight finished *first* in the obstacle course! They are now in the lead with three points!"

There was a lot of applause, and the campers from Cabin 8 gave each other high fives. Kenny and Mitch went to congratulate the winning counselor, who looked proud and happy.

"Cabin nineteen finished second, and Cabin two finished third." Arthur frowned with a puzzled look on his face as he made the next announcement. "For the first time in the history of Camp Bearclaw, *all* of the campers from Cabin thirteen finished dead last."

There were hoots of laughter, but Sabrina's campers stood stone-faced, as usual.

"We'll do better on the next event," she told everyone. She wished she really felt that way.

Half an hour later it was time for the canoe race, and Sabrina could barely stand to watch. Each cabin could enter one canoe with two rowers, one in the bow and one in the stern. She chose Rhonda and Linda to represent their team, thinking they were the biggest and strongest of her campers.

"Row as fast as you can," she told them slowly. "Try to go faster than the others!"

"Yes, Sabrina," Rhonda and Linda answered at the same time.

She quickly added, "But don't run into anything."

"Yes, Sabrina."

The teenager rolled her eyes. She didn't have much hope for her team.

To her surprise, Rhonda and Linda were not totally inept. Rowing a canoe was sufficiently mindless that they could do it, but they didn't realize the importance of steering, too. They rowed about twenty yards off-course, into the reeds, and missed the finish line.

The victors were two big eleven-year-olds from Jill's cabin, so those kids were now tied for the lead. The second- and third-place finishers also picked up some points. Sabrina thought about quitting, but the severe look on Arthur's face warned her that wouldn't be a good idea.

When they were walking back from the river to the camp, Arthur came over to Sabrina and demanded, "What are you doing?"

"I'm not doing anything," she answered. "Well, I'm watching my team get beat."

"You're throwing the games!" he whispered angrily. "In all my years at Camp Bearclaw, I've never seen such reprehensible behavior!"

Sabrina sighed. "We'll try to do better."

"You'd better," he said threateningly. "These are the *Pride* Games, not the Goof-off Games!"

But the next contest was archery, and they didn't do any better. In fact, not one of her campers could concentrate well enough to even hit the target with an arrow, let alone win the event. They finished dead-last again and were one of the few cabins that had no points at all.

At lunch in the Dining Hall the other campers snickered and sneered at her pathetic crew. They called them spiteful names right to their faces. Of course, her kids did nothing in return, because they were beyond caring. Sabrina got angrier and angrier, but she had to bite her tongue and say nothing. She didn't want to draw any more attention to her wretched weirdos.

The first event after lunch was the tug-of-war, and she was certain that her kids would be good at that. They would *love* to drag a bunch of other kids into the dirt! With Rhonda to anchor them, they had a good chance of winning. But they would never win anything as long as they were zombies.

While the other campers and counselors were finishing their lunch, she took her crew out the kitchen to hang out by the garbage cans. That was where they belonged.

"We can't go on like this," Sabrina muttered to herself. She glanced at a clump of suspicious-looking weeds and snapped her fingers. "Hey, maybe if I gave all of us *poison ivy!*"

"Yes, Sabrina," her campers answered in a mono-tone.

The witch sighed. "No, that's not a solution. Why can't I just admit that we're sunk?"

Suddenly she saw a flash of something furry, black, and small in the forest. It darted between the trees and stopped at the edge of the woods, crouching under a bush. Sabrina looked around and saw Arthur standing in the kitchen doorway, spying on them. As weird as they were acting, she supposed she couldn't blame him.

When Arthur saw that he had been spotted, he ducked back into the kitchen. Sabrina was glad that Salem had taken a moment of precaution. She sneaked over to the edge of the forest and crouched down beside the black cat.

"What's up?" she asked. "I thought you were sleeping today."

"I suddenly got an idea how to reverse the spell," said Salem. "It's an old trick I had forgotten. You know, ever since I was wrongly stripped of my powers, I can't remember much about magical spells."

"What is it? What!" asked Sabrina desperately.

The cat purred. "If you can remember exactly what you said that fateful night—and repeat it backward—you just might reverse the spell."

Sabrina sat on the grass beside him and frowned thoughtfully. "A hundred times since then, I've thought of how stupid those words were. I think I can remember them. Let me see, it went like this:

"From now on, you will obey
Every little word I say.
Don't talk back or cause a crime;
You'll be perfect all the time.
All of you will think as one;
You won't have any more *fun!"*

"That is certainly what happened," remarked
Salem. "Now say it backward. And *mean* it."

Sabrina nodded determinedly. Using her witch's
skill with words, she said,

"Nuf erom yna evah t'now uoy;
eno sa kniht lliw ouy fo lla.
Emit eht lla tcefrep eb ll'uoy;
emirc a esuac ro kcab klat t'nod.
Yas I drow elttil yreve,
yebo lliw uoy, no won morf!"

At the word "morf," she heard a grumble behind
her. "What's going on?" demanded Rhonda. "I'm
hungry!"

"Me, too!" groused Patty.

Alicia gazed at her empty hands, as if to ask,
Where's my video game?

Karen cried happily, "Look! It's the kitty!" She
rushed over to pet Salem.

Jenny looked around at the garbage cans and
demanded, "What are we doing out here? What
day is it?"

Sabrina clapped her hands with joy, and then she

quickly grew solemn. "Oh, girls, something terrible has happened."

"Like what?" asked Linda. "How did we get here? The last thing I remember is being in the cabin—"

"Yes, and you all calmed down and enjoyed the week. Now it's Friday, and we're in the middle of the Pride Games."

"I'd say you've been out in the sun too long," answered Patty.

"Okay," said Sabrina, "we're going back into the Dining Hall to get something more to eat. If you like, you can ask the other campers what day it is. Don't be surprised when they tell you it's Friday. But that's not the worst of it. In the Pride Games, you guys are dead last. Everybody has been kicking your butts."

"That's not possible," scoffed Patty. "We could take those bozos any day of the week."

"Yeah!" agreed the other girls.

Sabrina pointed to the kitchen door. "Go back inside and ask them."

"*I* don't believe you," grumbled Linda, leading the way back into the Dining Hall.

Sabrina watched them go, then turned and scratched Salem's head. "Good kitty."

"I know," the cat said smugly.

A few minutes later the campers of Cabin 13 were wolfing down second helpings of food, but they sat in stunned silence. They had asked around and had found out that it *was* Friday. Not only had they lost several days of their lives, but they had finished last in every event in the Pride Games.

"What I don't understand," said Sylvia, puzzled, "is how did we win the Talent Show?"

"That's not important now," snapped Rhonda. "What's important is that everybody's laughing at us—they think we're *geeks!*"

"So far, we've only done a few events," said Sabrina. "We have the rest of today to make a comeback. We can *win* these games, I know we can!"

The girls looked around at the other tables, where campers were still pointing and snickering at them.

"We're the laughingstock of the whole camp," muttered Patty. "We're like a *joke.*"

"What's the next event?" asked Linda angrily.

"Tug-of-war," answered Sabrina. "Eat plenty, because you'll need your strength."

Rhonda lifted her plate and shoveled the leftovers into her mouth. "Don't worry," she sputtered through a mouthful of food, "we're gonna drag their butts all over this camp!"

"Yeah," agreed tiny Karen, slamming her fist on the table. "Let's show this camp that Cabin thirteen is back!"

Sabrina sighed. She was never so glad to hear that.

Chapter 12

Sabrina had always liked tug-of-war. It was a very simple game—the team that was the strongest and wanted to win the most usually won. She didn't worry about competing against the boys' cabins, because ten- and eleven-year-old girls were usually bigger than boys of the same age.

Besides, it was awfully fun beating boys.

The counselors took the obstacle course apart, because they held the tug-of-war contests over the same muddy ditch. Not only would the losers be dragged across the line, but they would also be dragged into the mud. Like most of these games, the main point seemed to be to get kids dirty.

"To make it even," announced Arthur, "if one cabin has more kids than another, the one with more kids has to sit campers out. We must have the same number of campers on each end of the rope."

Sabrina noticed that the smaller kids were the ones forced to sit down and watch. Tug-of-war was a brutal sort of game, the kind that everyone wanted to win.

They watched a few matches, and then it was time for Cabin 13 to take on their first challenger. For a change, Sabrina felt confident. Her girls looked hurt and angry at the way everyone was making fun of them. They were ready to take out their frustrations on somebody.

The boys from Cabin 6 laughed at the misfits as they lined up on the opposite side of the rope. At the end of the line, Rhonda wrapped the rope around her waist and nodded solemnly at Sabrina. The boys had a big kid at the end of their rope, too, but he was laughing and goofing around.

Linda was in the front, and she dug her big feet into the packed dirt. Behind Linda stood Patty, Jenny, Alicia, Jasmine, Sylvia, Karen, and Rhonda as the anchor. All along the line the girls looked serious and determined. In fact, they looked as if they were still android campers, and many of the onlookers chuckled and pointed at them.

Arthur Rimbard gave Sabrina a disgusted look, as if he didn't expect much. "All right, campers, are we ready?"

Her crew nodded and braced themselves. They looked ready. The boys' team looked as if they weren't taking it seriously enough.

Arthur lifted his starter's pistol. "Ready, set, go!"

Her girls yanked hard, pulling half-a-dozen boys off their feet. The big guy at the end flopped onto his stomach, knocking down another kid. Pressing their advantage, her girls strained with all their might, and Rhonda chugged backward with her powerful legs. In less than five seconds they dragged a whole bunch of boys into a sea of mud.

As Arthur's whistle ended the match, Cabin 13 erupted in high fives and shouts of joy. They weren't zombies or misfits any longer—they were a team!

"Way to go!" screamed Sabrina. Now Arthur, Mitch, Jill, and many others were looking at her, and she grinned. "It's time to make our move!"

"Yeah!" shouted Alicia. Her teammates stared at the girl who had never spoken before saying this one word. She grinned sheepishly, showing off a shiny set of braces.

"All right!" yelled Sabrina. "Bring on the next cabin!"

The tug-of-war event was a straight elimination contest. If you lost any match, you were out. The winning team got three points, the second-place team got two points, and the third- and fourth-place teams each got a point.

A win would put Cabin 13 back into the hunt, because the points were spread out among a lot of cabins. Cabin 8, the leading cabin, only had five points.

They watched several more matches, which whittled the field down to eight cabins. One of them was Mitch's cabin, Number 3, and they looked tough. Jill's cabin was the only girls' cabin left, except for Number 13, and the girls had to face off against each other in the next round.

Jill's campers put up a good battle, but the monsters of Cabin 13 dragged them gleefully across the line and into the mud. Mitch's cabin won their next match, and there were two more matches. Now the field was down to four cabins.

Cabin 13's next match was so brutal that Sabrina almost used magic to help her team. But she knew that wouldn't be fair—they had to win it on their own. Besides, she had used enough magic for one week.

Somehow, her stalwart crew mustered enough strength to drag another bunch of boys, kicking and screaming, into the mud. There were weary high fives all around, but not much laughter. They knew their job wasn't over yet. Mitch's cabin also won, and it was down to just the two cabins, 3 and 13.

As the campers rested and drank lots of water, Mitch walked over to Sabrina, smiling. "I guess your girls were playing possum," he said. "They don't look like the same bunch who stumbled around the obstacle course."

"We're picking our spots," answered Sabrina. "We want to make it interesting."

"It's always interesting when you're involved," said Mitch. "Good luck."

"You, too." They shook hands, and his touch still felt warm and gentle.

Soon the combatants lined up across from one another one more time. It wasn't just Cabin 3 versus Cabin 13, it was boys versus girls. On the line were the bragging rights of being the toughest, strongest cabin at Camp Bearclaw.

Rhonda wrapped the rope around her waist, looking like a sumo wrestler. She was ready. Linda dug in at the front, and along the line the girls got their footing and a tight grip on the rope. Sabrina nodded to her girls and smiled. Win or lose, they were playing with all their hearts.

The boys were also deadly serious. They had seen this bunch of weirdo girls trounce two teams of boys, and they weren't going to let that happen to them. There would be more events later on, but the tug-of-war got everyone's blood surging.

Arthur gave Sabrina a satisfied nod, as if she were again on his good list. He lifted the pistol in the air and licked his lips. "Take your places."

The teams started pulling on the rope prematurely, and counselors had to center it again. "Don't pull until I fire!" shouted Arthur.

Everyone held his breath. The only sounds on the lonely field of battle were a few birds chirping in the trees. "Get ready," intoned Arthur. "Get set . . . go!"

With loud grunts the tuggers heaved on their ropes. Both teams had gotten a good first yank, and both teams kept pulling, even as they stumbled and strained with the tremendous effort. The audience pressed closer to watch the monumental contest. Girls screamed for the girls, and boys cheered for the boys.

Sabrina grunted and groaned right along beside her valiant campers. "Pull! Pull!" she yelled.

Mitch was on the other side, exhorting his troops. "Don't let them beat you! Pull!"

With clenched fists, panting for breath, Sabrina watched the grueling contest. For what seemed like several minutes, the two sides pulled back and forth, only budging the rope a few inches either way. Both boys and girls sweated and strained, dropping to their knees, pulling with all their might. It looked as if neither side would ever give in!

Finally it was Jenny who got a weird look in her pale blue eyes. She actually grabbed the rope in her teeth and yanked like a dog. The girls drew inspiration from this weirdness, and they all pulled harder than before. Very slowly the boys began to move, their feet slipping on the bare dirt. With a loud grunt, Rhonda took one mighty step backward and dragged the boys over the line.

The boys shrieked as they plunged into the grimy mud, and the girls of Cabin 13 kept pulling until every inch of the rope was on their side. All of the girls screamed for joy and jumped up and down. Jill hugged Sabrina, and the two of them bounced around like ten-year-olds.

"Wow!" exclaimed Arthur Rimbard into his megaphone. "The tug-of-war was won in convincing fashion by the campers of Cabin 13!"

"Gotcha!" yelled Patty at the gloomy boys.

Sabrina's girls tried hard in the swimming and diving events which followed, but they finished third both times. This put them two points behind the leaders going into the last event.

It had been a long day, and many of the campers were completely ragged out. That's why, Sabrina decided, that Arthur scheduled a rather relaxing contest for the last event—the horseshoe pitch.

Sabrina didn't think they stood much of a chance, but Alicia turned out to be a master at pitching horseshoes. In the final crunch, she got two dead ringers and a leaner to win the event hands-down. *Maybe all that video-game playing really is good for hand-eye coordination,* thought Sabrina.

Her teammates mobbed Alicia, lifted her onto their shoulders, and carried her off to the Dining Hall for dinner. Mitch, Jill, William, Kenny, and everyone else came over to congratulate Sabrina. It was unreal! She couldn't believe it!

Cabin 13 had won that ugly trophy.

Sabrina sniffled back tears as she plowed through the crowd, all of whom were eager to shake her hand. Winning was great, but she was crying because her campers had redeemed themselves. They had proved they were as good as anyone here, without having to escape, steal things, or play practical jokes. They weren't the rejects anymore.

When Sabrina got to their usual table in the Dining Hall, her eight dirty campers stood at attention and applauded her. They all tried not to cry, but tears of joy came rolling down. It had been a long time since any of them were champions.

In the dark forest Sabrina and her campers followed a hundred other kids and counselors up the path toward Bearclaw Rock. The only lights on the path were the white candles each of them held in her hand. The procession of lights winding through the woods was beautiful—like the scene at the end of the movie *Fantasia.*

Even Sabrina's rowdy bunch were quiet and respectful as they wound their way up the path. This was not the path that Sabrina had climbed with Mitch; this one was wider and more level. Still it took the two hundred people in Camp Bearclaw almost an hour to climb the path and assemble around the fire pit at Bearclaw Rock.

Behind the massive rock were wisps of clouds illuminated by a bright half-moon. In the middle of the fire pit was a glowing campfire, snapping and crackling and sending sparks shooting into the air. Somewhere high overhead, a hawk cawed softly. It was the perfect place to end the last night of summer camp for these happy campers.

Sabrina looked around at the crowd and saw William, the cooks, and the bus drivers, too. Everybody was there, finding a seat on the ground, on the log benches, or on the rocks. There was enough light from the blazing campfire that they could put out their candles.

She gazed across the campfire and saw Mitch and Jill on the other side, standing together. She grinned happily as she held his hand. It was clear that they had bonded while Sabrina was wrapped up with her campers, and that was okay with her. He wasn't really her type—she liked cute and funny.

After the audience settled down, Arthur Rimbard strolled in front of the campfire. The crowd hushed, and the darkness deepened. For several seconds only the crackling fire and the proud hawk spoke to the night.

Arthur had no megaphone or microphone with him, but his voice floated across the breadth of this magical place: "Campers and staff of Bearclaw Rock, welcome to our candlelight ceremony. I can tell you, we've had some excitement this week. In fact, I can't remember a more stirring session than this week's."

He smiled at Sabrina. "We've had our ups and downs, and more than our share of rain, but we were all teammates in the end. Most important, we've formed friendships that I know will span the miles and the tests of time. You'll always remember this week at Camp Bearclaw. I know *I* will."

Several people laughed softly, and Arthur cleared his throat. "At this time we always honor the cabins who have distinguished themselves. For the first time in history, the same cabin that won the Pride Games also won the Talent Show, which makes them the most honored cabin in the history of Camp Bearclaw. If there had been an award for food fights, they would have won that, too!"

When the laughter died down, Arthur held out his hand. "I'd like to ask Sabrina Spellman and the campers of Cabin 13 to step forward and receive their trophies."

"We all get trophies?" Sabrina whispered to Karen as they walked toward the campfire.

"You bet," said Karen proudly. "And we don't even have to steal them."

"Hey, this is better than detention," added Patty.

As warm applause echoed across the mountaintop, Sabrina and her girls lined up, grinning. An assistant rushed forward with a box full of trophies, and Arthur started handing them out. There was a big trophy in the box, which he saved for last.

"Sylvia, Linda, Alicia, Karen, Patty, Rhonda, Jenny, and Jasmine," he intoned as he handed each of them two trophies. "All of you have been coming to Camp Bearclaw for many years, and we know each other well. I'm pleased to see you up here, receiving these awards. Maybe this will be the beginning of a whole new attitude for you young ladies."

Rhonda burped loudly, which caused ripples of laughter in the throng of campers. Arthur frowned. "Well, maybe not. At any rate, you're being honored tonight. And I think I speak for all of us when I say that you showed true grit in that tug-of-war contest!"

There were rowdy cheers for the girls, and the applause grew deafening. Standing beside Sabrina, Sylvia whispered, "I wish someone would tell us how we won the Talent Show."

"Who cares?" responded Linda, waving her trophies over her head. "We won!"

Arthur motioned for the audience to be quiet, then he picked up the large trophy and handed it to Sabrina.

"Sabrina, you also made history. Never before has a new counselor at Bearclaw Rock coached her team to victory in her first Pride Games. Nor has a new counselor ever won the first Talent Show she directed. Some of your methods are a bit unusual, but no one can argue with the results. May I say, from all of us—welcome to the Camp Bearclaw family!"

Sabrina staggered under the weight of the trophy, and everyone applauded. Now she felt really guilty, because she still intended to quit tomorrow. Plus, she still had her pet cat sleeping in her cabin. But this wasn't the moment to get in trouble or make a scene. This was the moment to be gracious.

"Thanks," she said, hefting the trophy. "You've all been great to me, and I really appreciate this honor. I'm sorry I haven't gotten to know more of you, but . . . let's do this again sometime!"

There was more applause, and Arthur took the

gigantic trophy from her. He whispered, "We'll have that engraved with your name and put on display in the Lodge."

"Thanks," muttered Sabrina, still in a daze.

"All right!" crowed Arthur. "Who wants to sing 'Kumbaya'?"

Since the campers were exhausted from the day's strenuous activities, they all went back to their cabins after the ceremony and sing-along at Bear-claw Rock.

Cabin 13 was a little noisy as the girls settled down in their sleeping bags, but it wasn't nearly as bad as the first nights had been. And it was a lot better than the nights when they had been under the obedience spell. At last Sabrina had a cabin of regular girls.

Just before lights-out, the teenager was headed to her bunk when she heard a whisper: "Sabrina."

It was an unfamiliar voice, and she turned to see Alicia sitting up in bed. The girl's video game was nowhere in sight.

Sabrina knelt down beside the gangly camper and smiled. "Hey, that was great horseshoe tossing! It really nailed the victory down for us."

The girl smiled, revealing her shiny braces. Self-consciously, she covered her mouth. "Thank you. You know how you kept talking to me? Just because I didn't say anything, it doesn't mean I wasn't listening."

"I know," said Sabrina, patting her shoulder.

"That's why there are too kinds of people in the world—the talkers and the listeners. I guess you know which kind I am."

"Thanks for everything. I never won anything before today."

"You did it," answered Sabrina. "You and your teammates. Just remember the next time that you feel like escaping from the rest of the world, we *need* you."

"Okay," said Alicia happily as she scooted into her sleeping bag. "Good night, Sabrina."

"Good night, Alicia." The teenager stood and walked past Karen's bunk. She noticed that the small girl was already asleep, with Salem curled up under her chin. If only the girls had been like this the first night, they could have saved themselves a lot of hassles. But sometimes events had to play out in their own warped way.

Sabrina turned off the overhead light and lay down on her bunk. For the first time since coming to Camp Bearclaw, she felt satisfaction in a job well done. She finally knew what Aunt Hilda had meant when she was talking about working a job. The point wasn't the money—it was contributing to society, making other people's lives better.

She realized that she couldn't quit this job in the morning. But there was one more thing she had to do.

☆

Chapter 13

☆

The next morning lots of kids were crying. They weren't crying because they hated camp, but because they didn't want to leave. But the buses were in the parking lot, and the kids were packed and ready to go. They spent their last bit of money on souvenirs in the Camp Store, and they hurriedly exchanged telephone numbers and addresses.

Sabrina hung out in the Lodge until she noticed Arthur duck into his office. She took a deep breath—this was the time. She strode into his office and shut the door behind her.

"Ah, Sabrina!" said Arthur magnanimously. "Everybody has been talking about you his morning."

"They have?"

"Yes. Some of your campers came down this morning, asking to use the telephone. They wanted to call their parents to find out if they could stay *another* week."

Sabrina blanched at the thought. "Really?"

"We couldn't let them, of course, because we're all booked up. But the parents called *me* to let me know how thrilled they were. They haven't seen that much enthusiasm out of their daughters in years. But we've got another batch coming in this afternoon, ready for you to work your magic on them."

Sabrina gulped. She had worked enough magic on campers for one summer. "That's what I want to talk to you about," she began. "Unless there are some changes made around here, this is my last day."

Arthur blinked in amazement at her, then he grew angry. "I've never had a counselor come in here and demand that changes be made."

"Well, you've never had a counselor like *me*," she responded truthfully. "If you don't want to hear me out, I'll just leave on the bus. Bye."

When she started out the door, Arthur ran after her. "Wait, Sabrina! Wait!" He shut the door. "Okay, what are your demands?"

"First of all, no more Cabin thirteen. It's not fair for you to stick all the special cases in one cabin."

Arthur frowned. "Yeah, I was already thinking about that. But it will make more work for the other counselors."

"And more satisfaction for them when they turn those kids around."

"Okay," muttered Arthur, pointing to the files on his desk. "I've got time to change the cabin assignments. What else?"

"I want to be able to have my cat with me."

"What? Positively not!" Arthur looked suspiciously at her. "That big black cat is yours, isn't it?"

"He's a well-behaved cat, and he was a very calming influence on the girls in my cabin. I don't think animals are out of place at a summer camp. In fact, we need *more* animals, animals that aren't dead and in jars. Some horses would be good!"

Arthur put his hands over his ears and rushed out the door. "You're going to turn this camp upside-down!"

"That's my job," said Sabrina, following him. "Making things better for people. Do we have a deal?"

He pointed a finger at her. "If you weren't Super Counselor—"

"Ah, but I am," said Sabrina with a grin.

ABOUT THE AUTHOR

John Vornholt has had several writing and per-
forming careers, ranging from being a stuntman to
writing animated cartoons, but he enjoys writing
books most of all. He likes playing one-on-one with
the reader. John has written over a dozen *Star Trek*
books, plus novels set in such diverse universes as
Babylon 5 and *Alex Mack*. His fantasy novel about
Aesop, *The Fabulist,* is being adapted as a musical
for the stage.

John presently lives in Arizona with his wife,
Nancy, and two kids, Sarah and Eric, and he goes
roller-skating three times a week.

Send e-mail to John at: jbv@azstarnet.com